Ten Percent Magic

www.mascotbooks.com

Ten Percent Magic

For more information, please contact:
Mascot Books, an imprint of Amplify Publishing Group
620 Herndon Parkway, Suite 320
Herndon, VA 20170
info@mascotbooks.com

Library of Congress Control Number: 2022904821

CPSIA Code: PRV1022A
ISBN-13: 978-1-63755-352-7

Printed in the United States

To our amazing fathers, Dr. Richard Zapanta and Charles Alder, who taught us to give back and pay forward by the example they set every day.

And to our children, Westleigh, Rence, Sofia, Valentina, and Elias, who will pass on our family tradition of advocacy to the next generation.

Golf Course

TeRRaCe

One

JAX

"Where's the volcano?" I looked around the chem lab and didn't see anything but a pile of rags on a table by the window.

Zoe raised her eyebrows and stared in the direction of the rags. "That thing?"

She shrugged and looked down at her phone.

The closer I got to the so-called volcano, the worse it looked. "This is your idea of a safe container for the lava flow?"

"There's a Coke can in it," she said without looking up, "and the pot holders can handle the heat."

"You think this mess will hold up for our test run *and* for class on Monday?"

She finally looked up, but the stink eye was so strong I wished she hadn't. "There are plenty more cans and pot holders where these came from."

Having Zoe as a lab partner sucked. I'd known her since sixth grade and still hadn't found anything to like about her. "If this doesn't work, we're gonna fail."

She strolled over to the "volcano." "We're not going to fail. I'm telling you, the pot holders will work. When Chang's burned down, the only thing left were pot holders just like these." She proudly pointed to her rag dump like it was the Taj Mahal. "Where's the vinegar and baking soda?"

I pulled the containers from my backpack and set them on the table. "Vinegar, baking soda, and, for extra credit, sound effects, our secret ingredient."

She rolled her eyes. "Let's do this thing already."

That was fine by me. If I got out of here by three I could hit the skate park before work.

She held up her phone. "You pour. I'll record."

I dumped the pre-measured baking soda into the can and poured the vinegar on top of it. When it started to foam, I counted to ten before adding the sound effects, and then the volcano started making popping sounds. "It's working!"

Bright purple lava poured out of the hole in the rags, and when it hit the metal lab table, the popping sounded like gunfire.

And then the volcano exploded.

Zoe ducked just in time to miss being hit by lava-soaked pot holder pieces, and the room started to fill with smoke that smelled like rotten fish.

"Damn, Jax! You trying to kill us?"

My eyes burned and I was coughing so hard I doubled over to catch my breath.

She laughed. “You up for an Oscar? The smoke’s gone already.”

When I opened my eyes, the air was completely clear. “What the . . .”

“All that drama for nothing,” Zoe said, looking down at her phone as if none of it had happened.

The smoke wasn’t the only thing that was gone, though. There was no lab table, no mess from the explosion, and no sign that we’d even been in the science lab to begin with.

I shook my head, trying to wake myself up from this weird dream, but that just seemed to make things worse. “Zoe, pry your eyeballs away from your phone and look around.”

“One sec. I’m trying to get my texts.”

“Now.”

Sighing, she looked up, and when her mouth fell open I knew I had her attention. “What the hell? Is this a trick?”

“Yeah, the explosion gave me superpowers.”

“Save the sarcasm, Jax. I’m serious. Where are we?”

“How should I know?”

We looked around the room, which actually *was* round. It had a high ceiling and two huge windows on opposite sides of the room. In the middle of the room there was a round marble table, and the circular cabinet suspended over it was filled with labeled bottles. “Unicorn Tears, Eye of Newt, Snow Starter,” I said as I reached for “Star Seeds.” Inside the bottle, I could see tiny white lights swirling around. “Zoe, you gotta see this.”

She was looking out one of the windows. “No, *you* gotta see *this*.” She pointed to a snow-covered mountain crisscrossed by ski trails. “We are definitely not at school.”

I put the bottle back carefully, not wanting to cause *another* explosion, and stood beside her. She was right—we weren't at Garfield—but there *was* something familiar about the view. I pointed to a blue river. "That looks like the river in Critter Country, doesn't it?"

"Yeah, but if it is, Star Wars should be where that mountain is."

"But look over there. That's Tom Sawyer's Island."

She shook her head. "That still doesn't explain the mountain."

"The park's been closed for a while. Maybe it's a new attraction."

"Fine. Let's say it *is* Disneyland. How did we get here?"

Fair question, but I wasn't about to take the bait. Instead, I walked across the room and looked out the other window. "That's definitely Tomorrowland. That's good enough for me."

"*What*?" She came over to see for herself. "I see it, but I still don't believe it."

"You're losin' it, girl. If you can see it, it's real."

High-pitched laughter filled the room and bounced off the curved walls.

Zoe and I looked at each other to make sure we'd both heard it. We looked inside cabinets and behind shelves, but the only sign of another human was the silver hair clip that Zoe found on a chair that looked like a throne.

"This place gives me the creeps," she said, rubbing her arms. "And there's no Wi-Fi."

"So let's go." I headed for a round door that looked like a chocolate chip cookie baked for a T. rex.

"You have no idea what's out there!" She crossed her arms as if somehow that settled it.

"We have no idea what's in here either. All I have to do is make it to South Harbor and I'll be on my way home. You coming?"

She didn't budge. "See ya."

I shrugged and headed for the cookie door. Outside was a long hallway with an arched ceiling painted like a blue sky. The pillars holding up the "sky" were trees with chocolate-bark trunks and potato chip leaves. My stomach growling, I wondered if I could eat them but decided not to push my luck.

The hallway led to a silver door shaped like a four-leaf clover, but there was no handle. I shoved it and waved my hand in front of it in case it was motion-activated, but the door wouldn't open.

Damn it.

A place this big had to have more than one door. If the public exit was locked, maybe there was a door for employees.

As I was trying to decide where to look, I heard voices and darted behind a tree trunk. It was two clowns. They tap-danced by me and then right into what I thought was a mirror.

What the . . .

Since I didn't want to run into them on the other side, I counted to a hundred before I followed them through.

Now or never.

I took a deep breath and stepped through. And then the world went dark.

Two

-▽-

ZOE

When the chocolate chip cookie door closed behind Jax, I wanted to run after him, but I was too afraid to leave the room. I was too afraid to even *move*. What if what happened in the lab happened again and I had to be in the same spot to get back?

I closed my eyes and took a deep breath. Maybe I was dreaming and when I opened my eyes on the count of three, I'd be in my bed and Mom would be shouting at me to come down to breakfast. To make it more official, I counted out loud, "One, two," and then I heard the high-pitched laughter again and my eyes popped open.

The laughter was echoing around the room but seemed to be coming from the window. I forced myself to be brave, or at least act brave, and walked over to the window, thinking maybe the voices were coming from outside.

"Hehehehehehe."

I jumped back. The laughing was right next to me, but there was nobody there.

My mouth went dry and my feet were frozen in place. I wanted to run, but all I could do was stand there and stare at the empty space in front of me.

"Stop laughing, you're scaring her," one of the high-pitched voices said.

"You started it," another voice said.

I pinched myself hard enough to make my eyes water. "Are you ghosts?" I said, my voice quivering. Hearing myself sound so scared made me even more scared.

"Nooo," the two voices said in unison as the sunflowers on the windowsill shook their heads. "We're standing right in front of you."

"Um, are you guys, like, animatron flowers or something?" I couldn't believe I was attempting to talk to flowers, but as weird as everything was, what did I have to lose?

"This must be your first time here," the shorter one said.

"Where *is here*?" I asked, looking more closely at the flowers to see if they were mechanical.

"Ms. Ella's laboratory," the taller one said.

They looked real, but that wasn't possible. Aunt Regina was always telling me that if I didn't cut back my screen time, I'd fry my brain. Is that what happened? I'd gone and fried it?

"The real question," the shorter one said, "is how did you get here? Ms. Ella hasn't conducted an apparition experiment in weeks."

That's it, then. I've lost my mind.

"Actually," the taller one said, "I'm wondering the same thing, but we haven't even introduced ourselves." She bowed. "I am Fibonacci, named after Leonardo of Pisa."

The other one bent its head toward the floor. "And I am Fermat, named after Pierre de Fermat."

It was so sweet and silly at the same time that I had to laugh. "You don't have to bow for me. I'm Zoe."

"Welcome, Zoe," Fibonacci said. "What type of magic do you have?"

"Magic? Um, none."

The flowers chatted amongst themselves in a language I'd never heard before, but based on the inflection of their voices, I got the feeling they were worried about something. Like when Mom and Aunt Regina were talking and suddenly switched from English to Spanish. Finally, Fibonacci delivered the verdict.

"So the boy who left is the one with magic."

"Jax?" I laughed. "The only tricks he can do are on a skateboard."

Both flowers shook their heads. "It takes magic to appear in Ms. Ella's laboratory."

I shrugged. "We were doing a science experiment and it blew up. When I opened my eyes, we were here."

Fibonacci and Fermat started another discussion, so I took the opportunity to have a closer look around the lab. Between the marble table in the center of the room and the cookie door, there were three curved bookshelves that looked like rainbows. The books were organized by the color of their covers, from candy-apple red on the left to violet on the right, with all the other colors in between. It looked pretty, but I wondered how Ms. Ella, whoever *she* was, could find what she was looking for with this system.

The flower girls were still chattering, so I walked down one of the aisles, checking out the titles on the spines of the books. *How to Turn Your Ex-Boyfriend into a Toad, Flying by the Seat of Your*

Pants, *Conjuring 101*, *Dimension Traveling without Losing Your Clothes*. That one stopped me.

Seriously? What if I reappeared in the science lab and I was naked?

"Zoe," the flowers sang my name just as I was reaching for the book.

"We've decided that you should meet Ms. Ella," Fibonacci said. "It's not the normal protocol, but if you don't know how you got here, we don't know how to help you return."

"What *is* the normal protocol?"

"If you had magic, we'd send you to the Tower for orientation. I'm afraid we have no protocol for humans without magic."

I sighed. "Will Ms. Ella come here?" The last thing I wanted to do was find out what was outside. Inside was weird enough.

They laughed again. "She's already here," Fermat said, and they both tilted their heads toward the throne.

"Is she invisible?" I leaned to the right and then to the left to see if that would somehow make her appear.

The flowers giggled again and told me that Ms. Ella's office was at the top of the spiral staircase behind the throne.

"I don't see a staircase."

"It's made of crystal," Fibonacci said. "You'll see it when you're closer to it."

That wasn't any harder to believe than anything else that was happening, so I walked toward the throne, and when I was a few yards away, I could see something glistening behind it, the way moonlight looks on snow. Two more steps forward and there it was, a clear spiral that went up so high I couldn't see the top.

Oh. My. God.

I hate heights and as I started to climb, I felt a little queasy. I wasn't sure if it was the illusion of being suspended in midair or the chili I'd had at lunch, but I stopped for a minute to pull myself together. I was pretty sure puking wasn't part of standard protocol. Deep breaths. Once I felt confident that lunch was going to stay in my stomach, I continued up the stairs until I came to a glass ceiling. Not sure what else to do, I knocked.

"Is that you, Robin?" a female voice called from above.

"No, ma'am, it's Zoe."

The transparent ceiling slid open and I flinched when a scowling indigo face appeared above me, framed with a mane of rainbow-colored hair. "*Who* is calling me ma'am?"

"I am, ma—I mean, I didn't mean to offend you. Me and Jax just appeared in the laboratory and the sunflowers told me to see Ms. Ella."

"So you're Zoe." She shook her head and her rainbow-streaked hair rippled around her shoulders. "Well, come on up then."

When I stepped up into the room, I saw that the walls were as clear as glass, and like the laboratory far below, the room was round. There was sky all around, like I was standing on a cloud.

"I am Ms. Ella, and this is my dear friend Aly." She gestured to a tall thin girl who was sitting cross-legged on a silver sofa. She didn't look that much older than me, but I'd never seen anyone so exotic. Her eyes were the color of emeralds and her skin was ebony. "You might know her as Alice, from Wonderland."

"But Alice has blond hair and blue eyes and—"

"Not here, she doesn't. We choose our appearance and change it whenever we like. I bet you'll never guess *my* old name."

Aly grinned. "I'll give you a hint. Girls who wear glass slippers don't marry princes."

"*Cinderella.*"

They both laughed.

"You didn't marry the prince?"

"Of course not," Ms. Ella said with one hand on her hip. "What self-respecting girl would marry someone who was so self-absorbed that he couldn't remember what her face looked like?" She snorted. "Finding me with a shoe—please."

"I never thought of it like that."

"Well, it's time to think like you've never thought before," Aly said. "We have things to tell you that are much more remarkable than a girl turning down a marriage proposal from a pompous prince."

"Have a seat, honey," Ms. Ella said.

I sank into an overstuffed yellow chair and they attempted to bring me up to speed, but none of it made sense. I tried to keep it straight anyway because they were so *serious* about it.

According to them, we were in a dimension called Imagine where reality, including time, is flexible, whatever that meant. A while back, a great wizard visited Disneyland and liked it so much he made a new dimension that sort of looked like it and named it Imagine. But then a magician who called himself the "game master" showed up and started a game that combined virtual reality with magic, and that's when the trouble started.

I was starting to get a headache, and the sunlight streaming into the glass room was making it worse. I rubbed my temples, but it didn't help.

"We're making her head hurt," Aly said. "Listen, Zoe, there's too much to explain right now, but the crisis is that magic that's usually contained in the Magic Isle sector of Imagine is showing up in other sectors. We don't why or how to stop it."

I had no clue how to respond to a story like *that,* so I just nodded.

"Robin and Arthur should be here any time now," Ms. Ella said, peering down the spiral staircase. "What's most important is for us to reestablish the Magic Isle boundaries and restore reality elsewhere."

Just then, a tall guy with grass-green hair and beard stepped up into the office, followed by a shorter guy wearing a red cape.

"Robin and Arthur, this is Zoe. She's here to help us."

I am?

"Excellent," Arthur said.

"We can *use* some help," Robin said just before a map appeared in his hand. "I'll show you what I mean." He spread it on the table and pointed to the mountains. "That used to be Centauri's Edge, but the other day it became a ski resort."

"That's not the only change," Arthur said. He pulled a silver sword from an ornately decorated sheath at his waist and pointed to a river with it. "The Milkshake River is supposed to flow through Riskville, but it's taken to running right up High Street on some days."

Weird, but why are they telling me *this?* I pressed my lips together and tried to process what they were saying.

"The thing is, Zoe," Ms. Ella said, putting her hand on my shoulder, "we never know what's going to change or when. As long as your boyfriend is out there, he's—"

"He's *not* my boyfriend."

She raised her eyebrows the same way Mom does when I interrupt her. "I'm sorry."

"The point is," Aly said, "we can't predict when things outside will change or what will happen to your, um, to the boy you were with if a change occurs around him."

"I told him not to go out there." Everyone looked at me, but nobody said anything, so after an uncomfortable silence, I made the mistake of saying, "What do you want *me* to do about all this?"

They all started talking at once, and I could only make out a few words. Words like *magician, game,* and *danger.* Then Robin pointed to the map again.

"Future World and Centauri's Edge have been completely overtaken by magic, and the other sectors are starting to show signs of magic."

"Like the river in Riskville," Arthur said. "As far as we know, the only place that isn't subject to transformation is New Orleans. If Jax is there, he'll be safe from the game master but might run into other kinds of trouble."

My head was spinning. "How do we know he's even still in, um, Imagine?"

"Unless he's already made enough money to take a shuttle, he's here," Ms. Ella said. "Once we find him, we can figure out what to do next."

"Since New Orleans isn't in danger of transforming," Arthur said, pointing to it on the map, "that's the safest place for Zoe to look. And the sooner—"

"Wait—*what*? *Me*?"

"We can't go into the city," Ms. Ella said.

"As I was saying, the sooner we find the young man the better," Arthur said, sliding his sword back into the sheath.

Robin rolled up the map and handed it to me. "If it starts to get dark, head straight to the castle."

I looked at the four expectant faces surrounding me and swallowed the lump in my throat. "Is there anything else I should know?"

“Our version of New Orleans is mostly populated by animatrons and holographic images that look three-dimensional,” Aly said. “But some of the animatrons have been malfunctioning, so you’ll need to stay out of their way.”

“But if it’s as big as a real city, where should I start looking?” My stomach churned.

Aly held up a golden ball about the size of an orange and popped it open like a compact to reveal a mirror. “Show us Jax,” she said, looking into the mirror. As everyone leaned in, there was Jax, standing in front of an ATM.

“That’s the corner of Bourbon and Canal,” Ms. Ella said.

Aly handed me a small scroll. “It’s a map of New Orleans. I’d loan you my looking glass, but the magic only works for me.”

Arthur gestured to the spiral staircase. “After you, Zoe.”

My stomach lurched as I took the first step. If I puked on the way down, at least nobody would be below me.

Three

JAX

It was dark and I was flying down some kind of slide that curved around like a corkscrew. When I saw light at the bottom, I had no clue what was waiting for me, but I'd crashed my board a million times and I knew how to stay loose. *Chill. Chill. Chill.*

Brrrump.

I was spread out in a pile of something soft. As soft as dough.

What the . . .

And then I smelled sugar. *Sugar?* Like when they made *buñuelos* at Santiago's, the restaurant where I worked.

And when my eyes got used to the bright lights, it all made sense, if you can believe that.

I was lying in the middle of a box of marshmallows the size of a tractor trailer.

Well, this makes as much sense as a chocolate-chip cookie door.

I tried to stand up, but the marshmallows started moving around under me—*Damn, should have known*—and I couldn't get my balance. Then I felt the whole thing rush forward like my brother Trevor peeling out at a green light. *What the hell is happening?*

Like I used to do in the ball pit when I was a kid, I stretched my arms and legs out and rolled to the edge so I could grab the side and pull myself up. Just as I stuck my head up over the wall, though, I saw a tunnel racing toward me.

Shit!

I was in a boxcar!

I ducked just in time. Another second and I would have been flattened like one of those *buñuelos*.

The train made a few stops inside the tunnel, but I couldn't see anything, so I decided to stay where I was. I won't lie—I was wondering if I should have stayed with Zoe, but there was nowhere to go but forward now, so I made myself be patient. The train would eventually stop someplace where I could jump out, and when it did I'd be ready.

A few stops later, I started seeing some light and I got into crouching tiger position. As soon as the train pulled out of the tunnel, it slowed down and finally stopped in front of a factory. The sign said "Curious Confections," and I *was* curious about what they were going to do with all the marshmallows. But not curious enough to hang out.

The ground was a little farther down than I liked, but what choice did I have? Perching on the side of the boxcar, I locked in on a flat patch of grass and sprang forward like a cat taking down a mouse.

Aaah!!!

I didn't *think* I yelled out loud, but I wasn't sure. At least nobody else was around. When my feet touched the ground, I fell facedown. And when I opened my eyes, I saw that the green stuff I was lying on wasn't grass. It was sticky. It was . . .

Taffy.

It took a minute to get loose from the surface and crawl to what I hoped was a real sidewalk even though it looked a lot like graham crackers. As it turned out, it smelled like gingerbread, but it felt solid enough, so I stood up to try to figure out where the hell I was. Turning around in a circle, the first thing I recognized was the Temple of Doom. That meant I was in Adventureland, so if I followed the sidewalk that ran beside the train tracks, I should end up in New Orleans Square. Then I could hit an ATM for bus money and be on my way home. If I had my phone, I could have paid without cash, but it was in my backpack at school. Good thing my debit card was in my pocket.

I jogged past the temple and kept going until I got to an alley between a bakery and the French Market. I smelled sugar again, and my stomach growled for the hundredth time in the last hour. I'd take out enough cash for the bus *and* something to eat on the bus.

I ended up at the corner of Canal and Bourbon, and right across the street, next to the Lucky Lady casino, was an ATM. Finally, Lady Luck was on my side. But the intersection was filled with people on bikes and painted horses pulling carriages, and they were all going in different directions. So much for traffic laws. As I stood there trying to figure out if there was some kind of traffic pattern I was supposed to be following, two kids ran through me.

Wait—did they really just . . .

I didn't even feel it. How could they run right through me? Were they ghosts? Or something worse? When I turned around, they dissolved—for real—right into the crowd, and then a little girl with an ice cream cone walked through me.

Wait—am I *the one who's a ghost? Did I crack my skull when I hit the ground? What the hell?*

A man carrying a trumpet was heading toward me and I just stood there, waiting for him to walk through me too.

"*Oof.* Hey!" He'd bumped right into me, almost knocking me down. "Watch where you're going, dude!"

He just kept walking like he didn't hear me.

Before I could even try to figure any of it out, a bald guy pushing a stroller ran into me.

What is up *with these freaks?*

I backed up against the wall of the bakery to take a closer look at all these people who were doing their thing and not even noticing me. There was a guy wearing a chef's hat and a kid riding a bike and a woman with shopping bags in both hands. They *looked* normal, but after watching for a while, I noticed that the kids could walk through people and horses and even walls.

Ghosts or holograms?

Holograms didn't freak me out as much, so I went with that for now. But why couldn't the adults see me? Whatever the reason was, I'd have to start paying attention if I didn't want to be flattened for real before I got out of here.

Four

-∇-

ZOE

When my feet touched the marble floor at the bottom of the staircase, I was so relieved I wanted to get on my knees and kiss it. But the relief didn't last long.

"I'll walk you to the entrance of Riskville," Arthur said, "and from there it's just a skip and a hop to New Orleans."

"As a bird flies," Robin said, "it's only a quarter mile."

Once around the track around the football field. I nodded. My throat had that tight feeling like when I try not to cry, so I knew my voice would sound like one of Coco's squeaky toys. And thinking of my dog made my throat even tighter. He probably wondered why I wasn't walking him right now.

"Zoe?" Ms. Ella's voice snapped me out of my daydream. "Did you hear what Aly said about Canal Street?"

"No, ma—um, I'm sorry. I was thinking about my dog."

She sighed. "Oh, honey, I wish I could tell you something different, but the road ahead may be long and steep, and that doesn't even include the part about getting you back home." She gave me a long look up and down. "You need to forget all about home for now and put your heart into this search."

Aly put her hand on my shoulder the way my older sister did when I was scared. "You can do this. I know you can." A chill ran up my spine, and for some reason I believed her.

"Okay, let's get this show on the road," Ms. Ella said and swept across the room so fast that her rainbow hair streamed behind her.

We followed her through the cookie door and down a long hallway with a high ceiling that looked like the sky. After passing a bunch of giant trees with chocolate trunks, Ms. Ella stopped in front of a painting of a golden carriage. When she snapped her fingers, the carriage door swung open.

"*Whoa . . .*" What kind of optical illusion was this?

She giggled and gestured to the door. "Well, go ahead, Zoe. Don't be scared. High Street is just outside of the carriage. Get in—you'll see."

Arthur offered me his hand, but I shook my head. "You first."

He shrugged and stepped in, and I got in after him. We both slid across the purple seat cushion to the other side of the carriage, and sure enough, I could see a street just across the drawbridge. I followed Arthur onto the drawbridge, and from there High Street looked just like Disneyland's Main Street.

"Remember, Zoe," Arthur said, "if it starts to get dark, go straight back to the castle. No matter where you are, you'll be able to see its tallest spires."

"Okay, but what's the big danger?"

He stopped walking and turned to me. "After dark, the rules of the game change. The clowns can—" He shook his head. "Just trust me, and be back before dark."

Taking two steps for every one that he took, I was starting to feel faint from not eating. We passed the Market House and turned the corner at the ice cream parlor and were practically running by the time we got to the Riskville entrance.

"This is as far as I can go," he said. "Just cut through as quickly and quietly as you can. Once you're in New Orleans, you'll be safe from the game master, but keep your wits about you—there's other trouble there that a young girl can get into. And whatever you do, don't go into any saloons."

He was frowning and I could tell he wasn't thrilled about sending me out there alone.

"Look, Zoe, I wish I could go with you. But you're a smart girl—you'll be okay." He nodded like he was trying to convince *himself*. "Head right to Canal and Bourbon, where we saw Jax last, and then imagine where he would go next. He can't leave without a shuttle, so he has to be here somewhere."

I tried to smile, but I didn't have one in me.

As Arthur headed back up High Street, I remembered that I didn't know how to get into the castle. "Wait!" I shouted, my voice echoing off the buildings. "How do I get into the castle?"

"The same way we got out," he called over his shoulder without slowing down. "Just snap your fingers."

Just snap my fingers—great.

I *couldn't* snap my fingers. I could move my middle finger and thumb the way my friends did, but mine didn't make a sound. My *bff* said I had the silent snap, like it was a disease or something.

I shook my head to refocus, and just then two boys dressed in matching red shorts and white T-shirts ran past me. When I turned to watch them, I noticed that I could sort of see through them, like stained glass windows.

Holograms? Huh.

A giant tree house was up ahead and I ran toward it, thinking it would be like the Swiss Family Robinson's, but when I got closer it didn't look anything like it, except that it was built in a giant tree. Each section of the house was a different color, and the paint was peeling off in long strips that looked like dirty hair ribbons. The sign literally said Terrible Treehouse. I still wanted to get a better look, but there was no time for messing around.

Instead, I took the sidewalk that ran alongside what Arthur said was the Milkshake River and would take me right into New Orleans.

Wonnnk!!!

I jumped at the sound of a blaring horn and looked over to see a riverboat with "Mystical Mermaids" painted on the side. Instead of hippos popping up out of the water and elephants spraying water with their trunks, there were mermaids floating on lily pads and singing a creepy song. They sounded like whales.

"Zoe, come sing with us." One of the mermaids was talking to *me.*

The hair on my arms stood straight up. *How could an animatron know my name? Does the game master know I'm here?* Whatever the reason, I sprinted the rest of the way to the French Quarter. *Now, which way to Bourbon and Canal?*

I pulled out my phone and then remembered there was no Wi-Fi here, so I had to use the map to figure out where I was. If I was reading it right, I was only a few blocks from the ATM where we saw Jax, and I took off in that direction.

As I got closer, the streets got more crowded. At the Hard Rock Cafe, there was a long line of people outside waiting to get in, and I hoped Jax saw it, too. There definitely wasn't a Hard Rock Cafe in the real Disneyland, and maybe this would convince him that this wasn't Disneyland.

The smell of French fries made my mouth water. Maybe Ms. Ella would feed us when we got back to the castle. Did she and the other fantasy characters even eat? *Stay focused, girl. Only one more block to Bourbon and Canal.*

When I got to the intersection, I wasn't sure what to do next. The Lucky Lady Casino was on one side of the busy intersection and there was a Walgreens on the other side, but there was no traffic light. As I stood there wondering where Jax might have gone, a clown with a huge bunch of silver helium balloons crashed right into me, almost knocking me down.

"Hey!"

He didn't even turn around. I was about to call him out on being so rude, but before I could get the words out, a poodle and a young girl with brown braids ran through me. "Whoa!"

Being warned about the holograms and messed-up animatrons didn't make it less weird. I wondered what Jax thought they were. And where he'd go from here.

I looked up Canal Street, but my map said I'd be heading northwest if I went that way, and if Jax still thought this was Disneyland, he'd probably head east, looking for South Harbor. So I turned left on Canal and wove my way through the crowd, trying to avoid getting shoved again. After a few blocks, I could see water up ahead.

Is that the Pacific? Maybe there is *a way home!*

I picked up my pace and was almost sprinting when I saw him.

Jax!

He darted across the intersection in front of me and then disappeared through a revolving door. When I got there, the flashing sign said "Candy Casino."

Seriously? I wasn't old enough to go into a casino. On the other hand, Arthur said to stay out of *saloons*—he didn't say anything about casinos. So I went in.

Wow.

I was in a big lobby with a high ceiling and enormous crystal chandeliers. There was no furniture, and I was the only one in the room, which made me feel very noticeable. I tried to look casual when I walked to the archway on the other side, expecting somebody to show up and stop me, but nobody did. The archway was a rainbow of gumdrops, and when I squeezed one, it sure felt real. But hungry or not, I wasn't dumb enough to eat one.

In front of me was a long hallway with slot machines lined up on one side and a mirror on the other. The machines looked like adult-size gummy bears, all of them different colors, and the cushions on the chairs in front of them were giant marshmallows. I could see why this place was called Candy Casino, but why wasn't anybody here?

I walked past about twenty machines playing music and flashing displays, and the way the lights were reflecting off the mirror wall was starting to hurt my eyes. I was glad to see an exit just a few yards away, but when I got to the door, it turned out to be a 3D painting.

Or was it?

I tried snapping my fingers a few times, but they made more of a *poof* than a snap.

I must have missed something.

I walked back through the room and looked between the slot machines for another way out. The place had to be more than one long room.

If this is all there is, where the hell did Jax go?

As I was walking toward the lobby, a section of the mirror wall opened and a clown in a tuxedo walked in with a tray of shiny red candy apples. I could see that the room behind him was filled with people and I darted in before the door closed.

¡Caray! (Wow!)

Right in front of me was a mountain of cookies almost as high as the ceiling and more than twenty feet wide at the bottom. People were crowded around it, stuffing cookies into their mouths. Animatrons don't eat, so these had to be real people, and that meant the cookies were probably safe for me to eat. I stuffed a few in the pocket of my jacket, thinking I might need them later.

Besides the cookie mountain, there were blackjack tables and roulette wheels around the room, and a jazz band was playing on a stage along one wall. Then I spotted a row of tall glass tubes filled with every kind of candy I'd ever seen and some that I hadn't. The tubes were labeled, and people were getting the candy to come out by putting silver cups in the dispensers and clapping.

Clapping I can do, but where do I get one of those cups?

My mouth was watering, but looking around, I realized that everybody in there was an adult, and I was suddenly afraid that somebody would kick me out, so I kept moving. As I drifted across the room, though, they all ignored me. Maybe they thought *I* was a hologram.

At least nobody stopped me or asked me any questions, and I continued my search.

When I reached the very back of the room, there was a golden fountain as big as an elephant. And then I realized it *was* an elephant. It was shaped like the Hindu God Ganesh.

Amazing.

He had four hands, each one engraved with the name of a different-flavored milkshake. I wondered if my friend Sukanya would love this or hate it.

As I was standing there thinking about tasting the Butterscotch Bonanza, I heard some loud tapping to the rhythm of the jazz music. Not steady like a woodpecker—more like the rhythm of a dancer. Turning toward the sound, I saw the same clown that ran into me out on the street. At least it looked like the same one, although he wasn't carrying balloons. I watched him as he tap-danced through the crowd and right through a bright red wall.

Well, so much for doors.

I looked around to see how the people nearby were reacting, but nobody seemed to notice the clown or that a section of the wall had just opened and closed. Was this just something that happened every day in this place? And then I wondered something else: *Could Jax have gone in there?*

I noticed that if I squinted, I could just barely make out shapes on the other side—just silhouettes, no details. I could still hear the tapping, and then a bright light came on inside and the clown tapped into view right in front of me.

Shit. I jumped back in case he turned around and could see out through the wall the way I could see in. My gut said I should walk away, but when I noticed about a dozen kids sitting on a long bench, none of them looking happy, I couldn't.

More holograms?

Through the red glass, it was hard to tell for sure, but I thought they looked scared. Some of them might have been crying.

Those are real kids.

My mouth filled with the taste of metal, and I realized I was biting the inside of my cheek so hard it was bleeding. I forced myself to take a long, deep breath.

"Welcome to Candy Casino," the clown said to the kids in a sugary sweet voice. "You've won the chance to be avatars in our new game!" He tapped a few steps and spread his arms as if that would make his announcement more dramatic. "In a few minutes, you'll be taken to the candy ballroom, where you can eat as much candy as you want. And then our train will take you to the game room."

Game room or game master*?*

Maybe I was making something out of nothing, but that clown was seriously creepy, and something told me those kids were in trouble. I couldn't prove it, but I could tell Ms. Ella about it as soon as I got back to the castle.

Damn it, Jax—where are you?

Wondering where to look next, I heard someone scream on the other side of the red wall. The light wasn't on anymore, though, so I couldn't see anything. But then I heard something that made my blood run cold.

"¡Auxilio!" (Help!) someone yelled, their voice filled with terror.

Everyone around me was acting like they didn't hear it, but I couldn't have been the only one. I walked to the wall again and just stared at it for a minute, hoping an idea would come to me. Since clapping worked for the candy dispensers, maybe it would work for the door, too. But what would I do if it *did* open? If I got trapped inside, I'd *never* find Jax, and we'd never get back home again. But I couldn't just walk away.

Suddenly, the wall opened in front of me and I was face to face with the tapping clown. He was scowling. "Looking for someone?"

Does he know about Jax? "Um, no. I was just waiting for my mom. I thought I heard somebody in there speaking Spanish."

"This is New Orleans. People speak every language here." He tapped a few steps closer to me. His breath smelled like fish and the red lipstick around his mouth made his crooked teeth look even more yellow. Then he poked me in the forehead with his fat finger. "I don't believe you."

If this were L.A., one of the adults would have helped me, but they ignored this interaction just like they'd ignored the cries for help. I was on my own.

"Mom will be back in a minute," I said, buying time while I looked for an escape route. "You can ask her yourself." I smiled and waved to a woman standing behind him, and when he turned to look, I slid under Ganesh and out the other side. Then I bolted into the crowd.

"Watch where you're going!" somebody shouted somewhere behind me, and I didn't have to turn around to know the clown was following me.

Shit, shit, shit. Which way is the door?

I heard someone else shout, and my heart started racing. I knew I wouldn't make it out before he caught up with me.

WHERE'S THE DOOR!!?

By now all I could do was hide, so I ducked between a gray-haired man and a candy tube and spotted a towering "waterfall" that looked like blue licorice strands near the bandstand. My gut was screaming *Hide!* and I darted through the licorice and hit the ground hard. It was dark back here, but I could see through the strands. The clown was just a few feet away, turning around in a circle searching the crowd. Just as he turned toward the waterfall, somebody grabbed me from behind and clapped a hand over my mouth. *¡Ay, Dios mío! (Oh, my God!)* I was too scared to move.

The music stopped, and everyone stopped talking.

"I don't know where you're hiding, little lady, but we mind our own business here," the clown said loud enough for everybody in the room to hear. "If I see you again, you'll get more than a warning." Then he disappeared into the crowd and the band started playing again.

"Don't scream," the person holding me whispered. "It's me."

Jax?

He took his hand off my mouth, and as I turned my head he grabbed my hand.

"Run!"

Five

JAX

Dragging Zoe behind me, I sprinted through the crowd. Between boarding and boxing, I knew how to dodge and weave, but Zoe obviously didn't. Instead of following right behind me, she kept getting caught in the crowd, so I had to switch from holding her hand to clamping my hand around her wrist.

Just as we made it past the mountain of cookies, an alarm started blaring. Up ahead, I saw that the door to the lobby was open, so I put it in fifth.

"Faster!" I shouted at Zoe over my shoulder. If we didn't get through that door before it closed, we might not get out at all.

When the door started closing, I swung her around so that she was in front of me, and then I shoved her through the opening.

"Go!"

We tumbled through just before the door snapped shut behind us. The momentum was taking us down, but instead of crashing, Zoe did a somersault and landed on her feet. Somehow.

My landing wasn't as smooth, but within seconds, we were out on the sidewalk.

"We have to get to the castle before dark," she said. "Follow me." This time she grabbed *my* hand and started running down Canal Street.

After sprinting a few blocks, my chest was heaving and she wasn't even winded. I kept up with her, though, looking back every few steps to see if anybody was following us. I thought for sure she was going to run into somebody, as crowded as it was, but she carved her way through like a running back. Made *my* dodging and weaving look like nothing.

When we were at the corner of Canal and Bourbon, she ducked into the Walgreens and I followed. "Do you still think we're at Disney?" she said, glaring at me.

"I just saved your ass from a totally wack clown and that's what you have to say?" *Some gratitude.*

She wagged her index finger about an inch from my face. "Don't even. If you'd have listened to me and stayed in the castle, I never would have seen the kids, and the clown wouldn't have seen *me*."

"What kids?"

"The kids that were behind the red wall at the casino. Why'd you go in there, anyway? And why were *you* hiding?"

"I wasn't hiding. I was watching. Out on the street, people kept running into me and walking through me. I was trying to figure out where I was and what was real. I didn't see any kids or a red wall." *Was she wack, too?*

“Listen, Jax, I don’t have time to tell you everything.” She looked out the window. “We have to be back at the castle before dark.”

“Why?”

“Because the rules change after dark,” she said as if that made any sense.

“What rules?”

“I can’t *explain* it all now—I told you.” She unrolled a map and pointed to an intersection with her neon pink fingernail. “We’re here and the castle is over here. We need to cut through Riskville like this.” She traced the route with her finger.

“That’s twice as long as the river path.”

“But we can’t go that way.”

“Why the hell not?”

She pressed her lips together.

“If you don’t tell me, I ain’t goin.” I crossed my arms and took a step back to wait for her to give it up.

“How many times do I have to tell you I can’t explain everything right now? I’ll tell you later, *I promise*.”

“Just tell me why we can’t go the shortest way.”

She sighed. “One of the mermaid animatrons knew my name.”

“That’s weird.” Then I noticed that the Walgreens cashiers looked like robots. “But so is everything else in this place.”

“It might mean the game master knows about me.” Her voice was shaking. “Riskville isn’t safe because it’s part of a computer game that mixes virtual reality with magic.”

“I don’t know what the hell you’re talking about, but if it isn’t safe, we should get through there as fast as we can. And that means taking the quickest route.”

She didn’t look convinced.

"We'll run the whole way through and straight to the castle." I walked to the door. "Can we make it in less than ten minutes?"

We both looked up at the sky, which was turning dark. "We have to," she said as she darted out the door in front of me.

Three blocks down Canal Street, we crossed the bridge into Riskville. The streets were deserted. "You think there's a curfew?"

She slowed down to a jog and looked at me. "If there is, there's nothing we can do about it now, is there?"

I should have expected a smart-ass response. The street lamps along the river all turned on at once, and the river was also lit up from underneath. Dozens of mermaids were dancing on the water, balancing on the surface with their tails.

"Zoe!"

Yeah, one of them knew her, all right, and Zoe started running all-out again. I caught up, and we didn't stop until we made it across the drawbridge to the castle.

This time, she was gasping for air, too. She was also jerking her hands around like they were cramping up or something, and when the clock chimed she looked like she saw a ghost.

"What?"

"Snap," she said in between breaths. "*Snap your fingers*." She pointed to the life-size glass mosaic of a carriage on the wall.

I snapped my fingers with both hands, and the carriage door slid open.

"Damn!" Maybe we were both dead. Or was I hallucinating? Dreaming seemed too good to be true.

"This way," she said as she jumped into the carriage.

I followed her in, and when the door on the other side opened, we stepped out into the same hallway where I followed the clown through the mirror.

"Where are we going?"

"To Ms. Ella's lab. We're meeting with the magic containment coalition."

"The *what*?"

She just kept walking down the candy tree hallway. The ceiling that was blue sky earlier was turning purple, like the sun was setting inside, too.

"You said you'd tell me everything you know."

She stopped at the T. rex cookie door. "I know I did, but the truth is I hardly know anything. The coalition can explain it all better than I can."

She pushed the door open, and standing inside was a purple lady with rainbow-colored hair, a tall skinny girl with skin so black it looked blue, a dude wearing a red cape and holding a sword, and another guy dressed like Peter Pan or something.

It was official. I was hallucinating.

Six

-▽-

ZOE

When Jax saw the coalition standing there in all their colorful glory, his eyes doubled in size like a cartoon character's. Ms. Ella laughed out loud, so I figured it was okay for me to laugh, too. And then I couldn't stop laughing and pretty soon everyone was laughing, including the sunflowers. Well, everyone but Jax.

After a minute or so, Ms. Ella cleared her throat and we all got quiet. "Hello, Jax. I'm Ms. Ella and these are my friends Aly, Arthur and Robin." She made a sweeping "ta-da" flourish, the way models on game shows point to prizes that contestants can win. "Welcome to Magic Isle."

He looked at me. "Can you see them?"

"Of course I can see them. Why wouldn't I be able to see them?" I was starting to wonder if he'd hit his head or something.

He turned back to Ms. Ella. "Um, thanks."

"C'mon in, kids," she said. She walked past the rainbow bookshelves to the round table in the middle of the lab. The cabinet that had been right above the table was now way over our heads. The table was covered with a white linen tablecloth, and each plate had a different decoration. "We thought you might be hungry, so we set the table. What'll it be?"

Jax and I looked at each other, and my stomach growled so loud it sounded like a lion or some other big cat had snuck in. "Can we have *anything*?" I asked, wondering who did the cooking around here and, more important, how long it would take.

Aly smiled. "We don't call this Magic Isle for nothing."

The possibilities paralyzed my brain for a second. A serious foodie, I read the menu before I go out to eat, and I almost always order something I've never had.

"How about a pizza with extra cheese?" Jax said.

Ms. Ella snapped her fingers and a pizza the size of a car tire appeared on the table.

¡Fantástico! (Fantastic!)

Jax's mouth fell open and everyone started laughing again, but this time he joined in.

"Have a seat, everyone," Ms. Ella said. "Wherever you like."

I sat across from Jax and the others took seats around us.

"Have you decided what you'd like, Zoe?"

The pizza looked great, but what kind of foodie would I have been if I settled for pizza when I could have *anything*? "I've always wondered what pumpkin ravioli taste like," I said. "If it's not too much trouble, I mean."

This time, instead of snapping, she picked up her glass water goblet and held it high over the table. Then she drew three imaginary circles in the air with the glass while saying, "Ooey gooey, soft not chewy." A big puff of orange steam appeared in front of me, and when it cleared, a silver platter heaping with ravioli appeared next to the village-size pizza. I was so hungry I was afraid I'd start drooling, but I knew it wasn't polite to start eating before everyone was served. Instead, I unfolded the white napkin next to my plate, put it on my lap and pretended to wait patiently for everyone else to get their food.

Aly asked for vegetarian chartreuse, and Ms. Ella lifted her fork and spoon and left them just hanging there in the air by themselves. I'd never heard of chartreuse, but it sounded French so I couldn't wait to see what appeared. When Ms. Ella clapped her hands twice, the spoon and fork did a little dance together a few feet above the table. When the dance ended, the utensils drifted down to the table and something that looked like a cabbage cake appeared. *Pretty, but questionable.*

"It's a mix of cremini and white mushrooms, organic spinach and vegan crème fraiche," Ms. Ella said to Aly. "Just how you like it."

Arthur ordered "the usual," and Ms. Ella rubbed her hands together and a ginormous chef salad appeared, along with a loaf of garlic bread glistening with golden butter. *Oh my God.* My mouth watered and I put my hands over my stomach, trying to muffle the beast inside.

"And for you, Robin?"

He looked around the table. "What do you think? Baked Alaska? Chocolate éclairs? Apple pie à la mode?" His eyes landed on me.

I really wanted to try baked Alaska, but it didn't seem fair to Robin for me to make his choice for him. "They all sound amazing."

"Oh, what the heck," Ms. Ella said. She clapped twice, snapped her fingers once and all three desserts materialized out of thin air like everything else. "Let's eat, drink and be merry!"

By the time she'd "made" everyone's dinner, there was some kind of buzz in the air, like an electric current. The hairs on my arms were standing almost straight up. I didn't know if it was from all the magic or if maybe I was just lightheaded, but I took a few sips of water and hoped we got to eat before I fainted.

Ms. Ella held up her hands with her palms facing the high domed ceiling. "Thank you to Mother Nature and everyone who collaborated in the production of this meal."

Since she'd made the food with magic, I wasn't sure what she meant, but when the others nodded, I did, too. She smiled and lifted her crystal goblet, casting rainbows all around the room. "Here's to the success of our coalition and to our newest members, Zoe and Jax."

Since she was toasting Jax and me, I didn't know if I should lift my glass, but Jax lifted his and he worked at a fancy restaurant, so I figured he knew what he was doing. We all clinked glasses and then, thank God, Ms. Ella dipped her spoon into her soup. "Bon appétit!"

The ravioli melted in my mouth. For real—I didn't have to chew it. It just dissolved like butter. And everything was served family style, so I got to taste every single thing. And every single thing, including Jax's pizza, would have beat Bobby Flay.

"Normally, I'd wait until after dinner for business talk," Ms. Ella said as I was trying to focus on savoring it all, "but since magic is finding its way into so many sectors of Imagine, we don't have much time for small talk."

She went on to bring Jax up to speed on everything they'd already told me, and we both had questions. How did the game work exactly? What was the coalition doing to try to contain the spread of magic? And the million-dollar question: What could Jax and I possibly do about any of it?

The coalition members exchanged glances.

Ms. Ella smiled, but her eyes weren't in it. "The truth is, honey, we don't exactly know yet. For now, keeping your eyes and ears open in New Orleans will be helpful."

I nodded. It didn't seem like we had a choice.

"And as I explained, we can't try to send you home until we contain the spread of magic because we don't know if the corrupted magic can travel with you back to Earth. If it did, *anything* could go wrong. By helping us, we can all accomplish our goals faster."

"If the dark magic goes with you," Aly said, "it could spread like a virus through your world."

That didn't sound like the worst thing to me. Had to be better than the real virus we'd suffered through.

"It may not sound like the worst thing," Ms. Ella said as if she'd read my mind, "but when this kind of magic runs amok, it can create horror that you don't even want to know about."

Then I remembered what I'd seen. "I might have seen something bad going on in Candy Casino."

Everyone looked at me. "I saw a bunch of kids in a back room, and there was a clown saying something about taking them to the gaming room."

"How do you know they weren't holograms?" Aly said.

"Some of them were crying, and one of them shouted '¡Auxilió!'" (Help!)

Ms. Ella raised her eyebrows. "That can't be good. We'll have one of our connections look into it right away."

"Um. That's not all. A clown saw me looking at the kids and chased me. He said if he ever saw me again, he'd do more than warn me."

Arthur's eyes turned from brown to red. "Was the clown wearing tap shoes?"

"Yeah." *How did you know?*

He stood up and started pacing. "I told that bas-, that abomination that if I ever see him on Magic Isle, his dancing days will be through."

"You know him?" I said. New Orleans didn't seem like *that* small a place.

"Let's just say I had the displeasure of making his acquaintance when he tried to sneak across the border onto High Street."

"What do you think he meant about taking the kids to the game room?" Jax said. "Will he make them part of the game you told us about?"

"The avatars in the game are kids who are playing at home," Robin said. "The game makes an obscene fortune, but nobody's forcing them to play."

"Maybe not," I said, "but somebody was forcing the kids I saw to do *something*. There were no adults with them, just that creepy clown, and some of them were crying."

"Plus," Jax said, "if something wasn't going down, why'd the clown freak when Zoe saw those kids?"

Ms. Ella sighed. "Aly, can you locate the clown in question in your looking glass?"

Aly pulled out her mirror. "Show me the tap-dancing clown." She held the mirror face up in the center of the table so we could all look into it. A few seconds later, the clown's disgusting yellow teeth filled the frame. "Zoom out," Aly said. The teeth got smaller and we could see the whole clown. Then I gasped.

Behind him, little kids shuffled by, shackled together at the ankles.

Ms. Ella reached out and patted my hand. "Don't you worry, little lady, we will get to the bottom of this immediately. Fibonacci, please message the mayor and ask her to meet me on my secure crystal ball channel." She stood up and looked at me. "Before I go upstairs, we need to change your appearance."

I must have frowned because she added, "Don't worry, I can change you back before you go home. What's your pleasure? Do you have a favorite color?"

"Really?"

"Really." She smiled. "You don't have to choose a different color, but we have to make enough alterations for you to be safe in New Orleans until we can send you home."

The idea of getting to choose how I was going to look was the craziest thing yet, but what the heck—might as well go all out. "How about turquoise skin, violet eyes and long black shiny hair?"

Jax rolled his eyes.

Before I could make a smart remark, my skin turned turquoise. "Whoa." Even though it was my idea, it was shocking to see it happen. Aly turned me toward the windows and I saw my reflection. I definitely didn't look like me. But I did look oddly beautiful.

"That'll fool the clown," Jax said, "but what about that mermaid?"

"*What* mermaid?" Ms. Ella narrowed her eyes at me.

"An animatron in Riskville," I said. "It called my name."

Ms. Ella rubbed her arms as if a cold breeze was blowing through the room. "The mermaids aren't animatrons. They're real."

Now it was my turn to rub my arms.

"You two will stay here tonight," she said. "Tomorrow when you go back to New Orleans, take the long way through Riskville."

I glared at Jax. "Told you we should have gone that way."

He shrugged. "How was I supposed to know?"

"How come she knows my name?" I felt my heart starting to race like right before a gymnastics competition.

"She must have heard me say it," Arthur said. "I forgot how good their hearing is."

"I thought she was part of the game and if she knew I was here, the game master would, too. Does this mean the game master *doesn't* know I'm here?"

Ms. Ella sighed again. "Not necessarily. I need to dash upstairs for my meeting. Will you guys explain it to them?" She didn't wait for an answer before heading toward the crystal staircase.

The other coalition members all started talking. They agreed that if the game master knew we were here and was asking around about us, he probably didn't know our names, so it probably didn't matter that the mermaids knew mine. If he *did* know my name, the mermaids could tell him they'd seen me, but no one could think of a good reason why they would.

"Like us," Robin said, "the mermaids have free will."

"But that doesn't mean the game master doesn't know you're here," Arthur said.

"How can we find out?" Jax said.

"We can't," Aly said. "And that's why it's not safe for you kids to stay here more than one night."

"If he knows you're here and you're not showing up on any of his game grids, the castle is one of the first places he'll send his minions to look for you," Arthur said.

"*Minions*?" Jax said. "So why's it safe to stay here *tonight*?"

"It's safer inside than out," Robin said. "The rules change at night."

Same thing Arthur said.

"Where *is* the game master?" I asked, not sure if I really wanted to know.

"That's one of the things we've been trying to figure out," Aly said.

"Right now, we have more questions than answers," Robin said as he rubbed his green beard. "We should get some sleep. First thing tomorrow, Ms. Ella will meet with you to talk about finding jobs and renting an apartment in New Orleans. That's where you'll need to live until we contain the magic."

"Live?!" I blurted out. "I have a gymnastics meet this Saturday! If I don't make it home by tomorrow, my mom will have a heart attack from worrying. She probably already called every hospital in L.A."

"Zoe, time works differently here," Aly said. "Days in this dimension can be mere seconds on Earth." She cupped my chin in her ebony hand. "I know you're worried about your mom and those kids you saw and how you're going to get home and a million other things, but if you and Jax are going to get through this, you have a lot to learn and you have to learn quickly. If feeling sorry for yourself or worrying about your family could help, I'd be all for it. But it can't."

I was too tired to argue. "Can I ask one more thing before you show us where we're sleeping?"

"Sure. Let's talk on the way up." She walked to the staircase.

Not this again. I followed her up the spiral, which was illuminated by soft blue light. Everything else was dark, and since I couldn't see down, it wasn't as scary this time. "So, about that mermaid?" My voice echoed. "If knowing my name doesn't mean she'll rat me out to the game master, why doesn't Ms. Ella want us to take the shortcut through Riskville?"

Aly stopped on a landing that hadn't been there when I climbed up to Ms. Ella's office the first time. There was a door on both sides of the landing, and when she snapped her fingers both doors slid open. In one room, the walls were painted with a bunch of dudes that looked like superheroes, and the other was decorated like the inside of the bottle in the *I Dream of Jeannie* reruns.

I couldn't believe it. "Amazing."

Jax tilted his head toward the dudes. "Mind if I take this one?"

I laughed. "It's all yours." I stepped inside Jeannie's "bottle," and for the hundredth time that day I felt like I was dreaming.

"Get a good night's sleep," Aly said. "If you need anything, there's a bell next to the bed."

"Wait," I said. "Why should I be afraid of the mermaids?"

She stood on the landing for what felt like forever. "You should *not* be afraid of the mermaids," she finally said. "That won't help. But you should know that if you hear them call your name often enough, it will be impossible to resist joining them."

Before I could ask anything else, the door closed between us.

Seven

-△-

JAX

It was so bright when I woke up that I had to squint, but that didn't keep my eyes from watering. Everything around me looked blurry, and it looked like the life-size image of some red dude was swinging his anvil. I rubbed my eyes and looked at the other action figures on the walls.

Holy shit.

They were *all* moving. Except for the one who was missing. In the middle of the wall, where a green giant with an ax had been standing next to a lion last night, there was only the lion, which had blazing eyes and jagged teeth that looked way too real. Keeping an eye on him, I put one foot on the floor. Then a bell chimed and the lion looked right at me as if he'd just found his next meal.

"Good morning, Jax," he said. "Breakfast is in one hour."

"Uh, I'm not on the menu, am I?" I still hadn't put my other foot on the floor.

"Ms. Ella is not a cannibal." He sharpened one of his claws between his teeth.

"I was talking about you. How do I know you're gonna stay where you are?"

He yawned. "Only the heroes can leave their posts, so you have no need to be afraid of me."

He could have easily attacked me while I was asleep, so I figured he was telling the truth and got out of bed.

"You will find clean clothes in the closet next to the bath."

"Um, thanks."

I still kept an eye on the cat as I sprinted to the bathroom and locked the door behind me. In the center of the room, steam was rising from a sunken bathtub big enough to hold a baby elephant, but I was more interested in the window. Now that I knew this wasn't Disneyland, I wanted to get a good idea of what was really out there, especially New Orleans. It looked like a big slice of pizza with everything. You could fit two Disneylands inside it. But what was really crazy was that the rooftops were bright neon colors and every shape you could imagine—circles, squares, rectangles, triangles, hexagons, decagons and shapes that I was pretty sure didn't have names. *Wild.* It looked like CGI, and staring at it made me dizzy. The only buildings that stood out were a tall skinny clock tower close to High Street and a lighthouse by the river.

Seeing the river made me wonder where it led. Didn't rivers feed into the ocean? And if they did, wasn't it possible that the blue one led to the Pacific and back to L.A.?

I figured I'd ask the coalition at breakfast, but I needed a shower first. I stepped into the white marble shower stall, and the wall was covered with shower heads all pointing in different directions. Instead of faucets, there was a row of buttons, but none of them were labeled. *Great.* When I pushed the first button, it felt like somebody was aiming a fire hose at me and I jumped out of the way.

Damn.

I pushed the button again and the water stopped. The second button wasn't much better, though. All of a sudden I got hammered by hot jets of water that felt like needles and I shut that one off, too.

There was one button left, and at this point what did I have to lose? When I pressed it, hot water came right out of the ceiling, but not so hot that it burned. There was no shower head, just hundreds of tiny holes, like I was standing in the rain.

Perfect.

After I was done, I dried off with a towel as thick as a pillow and made my way to the walk-in closet. Just like the lion said, it was filled with clothes—jeans, shorts, T-shirts and even a pair of Nike Airs—and they were all my size.

There were also some dress clothes and a black roller-bag suitcase with a note that said I was supposed to pack everything I wanted to keep. There were almost as many clothes here as I had in my closet at home. But what blew my mind was the Exkate–X27 leaning against the wall. Nobody I knew had one of these boards. Not even the rich kids.

After I packed, I tucked the board under my arm and rolled the stuffed bag into the bedroom. The giant was standing next to the lion and actually bowed to me.

"Breakfast will be ready in fifteen minutes." He scratched the top of the lion's head. "I trust you found everything you needed?"

"Uh . . . yeah."

“Fantastic.” He clapped his hands together. “Leave your bag on the landing and Ms. Ella will send it to the lab.”

“Okay.” I felt too crazy to stand there talking to a painting, and having an audience of superheroes just made it worse, so I decided to go to breakfast early. “Thank you,” I said as I wheeled my bag out onto the landing. As I closed the door behind me, I heard the whole crew say “you’re welcome” at once. I believe in being polite, but this seemed a little ridiculous.

There was a purple roller bag in front of Zoe’s door, so I parked mine next to it. I thought about sliding down the spiral banister, but since I didn’t check it out for smooth ride clearance on the way up, I didn’t want to chance it. Instead, I took the stairs two at a time, and I was down in the lab in less than five minutes.

The new turquoise Zoe was lifting the lid of a silver dish on the counter next to the sunflower sisters.

“Hey, Jax.” She barely looked up.

There were a dozen covered dishes, and I wondered how long it would take her to decide. I didn’t want to stare at her, but it was hard to look away. The black hair and the turquoise skin were sort of an amazing mix.

One of the sunflowers giggled. “Good morning, Jax.”

“Good morning, Fib—”

“Fermat,” she corrected.

“Good morning, Fermat and Fibonacci.”

Zoe was still lifting lids and putting them back down, and so far the only thing on her plate was a croissant. I picked up a plate and loaded it up with scrambled eggs, pancakes, two thick slices of ham and a bowlful of cherries.

“Ms. Ella said you should begin breakfast without her,” Fibonacci said.

"She'll be here shortly," Fermat added.

I sat down and dug in, and after a while Zoe sat across from me with a mound of hash browns, a plate of bacon and a melon ball salad.

"You sure don't eat like a gymnast," I said between bites.

"How should you know how a gymnast eats?" She shrugged. "A girl's gotta keep up her strength."

I wasn't going to start my day by arguing with her, so I kept my head down and worked my way around my plate.

Ms. Ella arrived a few minutes later with our luggage hovering behind her. "Good morning, Zoe and Jax!" She handed us both a notebook and a pen. "Today you're going to write down your goals, and then it will be up to the two of you to figure out how to achieve them."

"You mean, goals about containing the magic?" I said.

"Well, no." Ms. Ella sat between us. "You might be able to help with that when you understand more about how this dimension works, but for now I want you to make a list of what you need to do to survive—and, ideally, thrive—in New Orleans."

Zoe clicked her pen a few times. "You mean like find a place to live?"

"Yes, but *finding* a place is the easy part. There are hundreds of apartments for rent." She tapped her own pen on a yellow legal pad. "But to afford even the most modest one, you'll need to show you have an income, and that means getting a job, and to get hired—" She stopped and looked at us. "You may want to write these things down."

I opened my notebook and scribbled:

1. Job/$

I looked back up at Ms. Ella. "You said, 'to get hired.'"

She tapped her pen on the legal pad again and smiled. "What do *you* think you'll have to do to get hired?"

"Make résumés, do research to find out what places might hire us, dress right for the interviews," I said.

"Write those down." She turned to Zoe. "Why aren't you writing anything down?"

"I'll write down the stuff that I might not remember. So far, everything is just common sense, isn't it?" She flipped her hair over her shoulder.

Ms. Ella raised her eyebrows. "Common sense is not the same as common practice. Surely you know that writing down your plans and goals exponentially increases your chances of achieving them. Do you think I became a chemist and built a multimillion-dollar company just by *thinking* about what I needed to do?"

Zoe opened her notebook. "Should I write down the same things that Jax is writing down?"

"Those and your own ideas, too."

I turned my notebook upside down so Zoe could read my list.

"What else can you add to the list, Zoe?" Ms. Ella said.

"How about, practice for the interviews? Like role-playing?"

"Very good. Write it down."

When Ms. Ella seemed to be satisfied with our lists, she said that our second challenge would be to rent a suitable apartment without getting ripped off. We were supposed to research apartment rental, find out about rates and leases, and write up a plan about where we'd look for a place and how we'd pick one.

But what were we supposed to do in the meantime? As swank as the room upstairs was, I could only take so much of superhero roommates and chatty lions. Besides, Robin said something about it not being safe for us to stay here.

"Of course, we can't have you living on the streets in the meantime," Ms. Ella said as if she read my mind—again—"so you can stay at one of my rental properties for the first month. You'll need to find something much less expensive, but Château Magique is next to the river, and that's where the best shops and restaurants are, too, so jobs in that district will pay more." She pulled two silver keys out of thin air and handed one to each of us. "The address is 1001 Wanderlust Boulevard."

We both wrote it down, and I read it back to her to make sure I had it right.

"Perfect," she said. "The pantry is stocked, but you'll need money for groceries, so I'm loaning you two thousand dollars. You can pay me back with monthly payments and 5 percent interest. How does that sound?"

I had no clue what a couple grand would cover in New Orleans, but we weren't in any position to argue. "How do we show you the plan we come up with for renting the apartment?"

"You can send it through Interland Mail, which is free. Or you can use the crystal globe in the rental to send an image. It's in the office, and there are instructions right next to it. You can also use the globe to call me, but the connection with the rental properties isn't secure, so be careful what you say."

"What *shouldn't* we say?" Zoe said.

Ms. Ella took a sip of water. "Well, if you don't want anyone to know you're working with the coalition, there are a whole lot of things you don't want to say. Globe-tapping is illegal, but there's no way to enforce it."

"We'll be careful," I said.

She nodded. "I am aware that neither of you are prepared for what you're about to face, so the less I help you, the better."

What kind of wack logic is that?

"You're going to have to use your brains, learn quickly and blend in. And most important, you're going to have to work together, and that means learning how to communicate with each other and cooperate. It's not about being right. It's about being effective." She stood up and pulled two plastic cards out of her pocket. "I opened a bank account for you. Since Imagine was fashioned after Disneyland, our money looks the same as yours, so you won't have to learn a new money system." She handed us both a card. "They work like debit cards in your world, but you only have two thousand dollars to spend, so before you buy anything, you need to make a budget."

"A budget?" Zoe said. "How can we make a budget if we don't know how much things cost?"

"How do you think?" I said, not wanting to look like an idiot. "We have to find out how much things cost and *then* we make the budget. Just like we have to find out about how to rent a good apartment before we start looking for one."

"Hmpf," Zoe said. "When did you get so smart?"

Ms. Ella cleared her throat. "Did you hear me say the words *communicate* and *cooperate*?" She put her hands on her hips. "I don't know what the problem is between you two, but you won't make it here if you keep acting like immature children. So whatever it is, work it out." She picked up her pen and her legal pad. "I think that's it for today."

"Ms. Ella." It came out like I had a frog in my throat. "About those mermaids."

"Yes?"

"Aly said if they called Zoe's name enough times, she wouldn't be able to resist joining them. Does that go for me, too?"

"That goes for all sapiens, but as keen as their hearing is, the mermaids can't hear you when you're in New Orleans." She smiled again. "Just remember to take the long way through Riskville, and don't use each other's names when you cross through."

A chill ran down my back, and Zoe's face turned a lighter shade of turquoise.

"From now on, I'm Chance," I said.

Ms. Ella swept her rainbow-streaked hair up behind her and tied it into a knot. "Honestly, the mermaids are the least of your concerns. I'll look forward to receiving your assignments in the next few days. I believe you know the way out."

Before we could ask any more questions, she was heading up the staircase.

Eight

-▽-

ZOE

I pushed the silver key into the lock and the door to the suite swung open.

"Whoa!"

"This is as uptown as it gets," Jax said as he wheeled his bag over the gleaming wood floor toward the window. "Check out this view."

The blue river, which would have been the Mississippi if this was our New Orleans, was so far below that the paddle wheel boats looked like bathtub toys. "This is way higher than the room I had in the castle. I wonder what floor this is." The panel on the elevator had just called it the "silver floor."

"Wild how this side of the river is stacked with high-rises but on the other side there's nothing but trees," Jax said.

"I guess." I was more interested in what was *inside* the suite. The living room was right out of the *World's Most Extraordinary*

Homes show. There was a burgundy leather sofa and chairs, a fancy chaise lounge and a coffee table that looked like marble. All the walls had paintings of landscapes, and on one wall, there was a framed map of Imagine.

"Come see the kitchen!" Jax shouted, making me jump.

"I know your momma taught you better than to yell inside the house."

When I got to the "kitchen," it was nothing but an empty room. "Where is everything?" My voice echoed off the smooth bronze-colored walls.

"Watch this." He turned to face the wall on my right. "Oven." Just like that, an oven appeared.

"Get out!" I was starting to get used to magic, but this was the coolest yet. "Let me try." I faced the opposite wall. "Refrigerator." And it was suddenly there, as if it had been there all along.

Jax stood next to the oven. "Countertop and appliances." A counter suddenly stretched the whole length of the room, and it had every kind of appliance I'd ever seen and some I hadn't. "A Vitamix!" Jax said. "We don't even have one of these at the restaurant."

"Just looks like a blender to me."

"You call yourself a foodie and you don't know this is the Cadillac of blenders?"

"Since when does a foodie have to know how to cook?"

"Since tomorrow," he said.

"Because I'm the girl?" I wouldn't have figured Jax was a chauvinist.

He laughed. "No, because I'm not doing it all myself."

"But my cooking skills are more like 'heating skills.'"

“That’s about to change.” He stood next to the refrigerator. “Sink,” he said and a deep porcelain sink with four basins materialized.

“I wonder if we can make *anything* appear, or just kitchen stuff.” I turned to the empty wall. “Bed.”

Nothing.

“Bicycle.”

Nothing.

“Okay, how about plates and glasses?” Cabinets lined the wall, and when I opened them, they were filled with china and glasses that looked like my grandmother’s real crystal.

Jax took out a glass and filled it with water. “Let’s hope it’s good. We don’t want to have to buy water.” He took a sip and smiled. “This might be the best water I’ve ever had.” He carried the glass into the living room and pulled his notebook out of his luggage. “I guess we better get started.”

“Our first day here?”

“That’s one way to look at it,” he said. “But we only have about two weeks to do everything on this list.” He opened the notebook.

“A month is four weeks, in case you forgot. I want to check out the restaurants.”

He shook his head. “We can’t do anything until we have a plan for doing the stuff on our list, starting with the apartment plan Ms. Ella wants us to do.”

I couldn’t believe it. Jax the school skipper was telling *me* we had to get to work. I wondered again if he had some kind of head injury, but I didn’t see any bumps or anything. I read once that brain injuries sometimes give people special talents, but nothing about making kids suddenly act like grown-ups. “What if we work on the research until six o’clock and then we go out for dinner?”

He rolled his eyes. “Zoe, we are not on vacation, in case you forgot. That stuff will have to wait.” He took out his pen and wrote something down in the notebook, but I wasn’t ready to give up.

“But we have to eat dinner.” He didn’t say no, so I kept pushing. “We could bring our notebooks. Make it a working dinner.”

He tapped his pen on the page a few times. “Until we figure out our budget, we can’t drop cash on restaurants. How about you pick a place that delivers and we each have fifteen dollars to spend?”

“*Fifteen*? Unless there’s a McDonald’s or Fat Burger here, we’re not gonna have too many choices.”

“Okay, twenty.”

“Twenty-five plus five to tip the delivery person.” I figured I could get something good for that amount. Not crab but maybe crawfish.

“Zoe, that would be more than fifty-five dollars—we can probably make three dinners for that much.”

“You don’t have to keep saying my name. I’m the only person here, in case it’s not obvious.”

The corner of his mouth twitched, but he didn’t say anything.

“After everything we’ve been through, don’t you think we deserve to have something nice our first night here?”

“*Everything we’ve been through*? The hard part is just starting.” He raised his eyebrows. “In case it’s not obvious.”

“Stop mocking me!”

“Stop being a spoiled brat.”

His eyes were smoldering the way my Uncle Ray’s did in the boxing ring. I took a couple steps back, just in case.

He walked out of the room but stopped in the hallway and turned back. “I know this is hard, but Ms. Ella’s right. If we don’t work together we might never get back home. That’s a lot more important than an expensive dinner.”

"A twenty-five-dollar dinner isn't exactly expensive. On Uber Eats, it's only one and a half dollar signs." I could feel myself pouting.

He got up and walked over to the window, turning his back to me. "My mom has to know I'm missing by now. She can't make it without me helping with the bills. I gotta get back home as fast as I can."

I knew Jax had been working at Santiago's since seventh grade, but I didn't know he was helping to support his family. "I'm sorry."

"Ms. Ella said we should cooperate. I guess we need practice." He was quiet for a minute. "If we each have twenty dollars to spend, we can get something like oyster po'boys or jambalaya delivered. When we get our first paychecks, we can go to any restaurant you want."

Part of me wanted to argue. Not because I disagreed but because I felt irritable. But I was also hungry. "Deal."

He punched his open hand with his fist. "So where do you think we should start?"

I was about to say something sarcastic but held my tongue. My family didn't need me to work, but I definitely wanted to get home as much as he did. "Maybe we can divide up the research for renting the apartment? Like one of us can look up locations and prices and the other one can find out about stuff we should look out for, like—I don't know—rats and hidden fees or something."

He laughed. "We should definitely look out for rats. Which one do you want to do?"

That caught me off guard. "Really? You're okay with me picking?"

"You pick this time, and I'll pick next time."

"Are you settin' me up? Maybe I should know what we're picking next time before I agree." I plopped down on the sofa across from the chair he was sitting in.

"We won't know what's next until we start doing the research."

"Fine."

He opened the notebook and set it on the coffee table in front of me.

Apartment Rental Research

1. What we need

   kitchen, bathroom, 2 bedrooms

2. Leases: Understand the big and small print

3. Location: Stuff to consider and look out for

"When'd you do this?" I'd been with him since Ms. Ella gave us the notebooks.

"When we were in line at the ATM."

"Oh." *Jeez, he doesn't waste time.* I reached for the notebook and pulled out my pen.

"What are you doing?"

"I'm adding 'living room.'"

"We don't need a living room. All we need is what I wrote."

"What about a laundry room? You planning to wash your clothes in the sink?"

"We can find a place that has a laundry room in the building."

"Okay, well, add 'laundry room in building' then."

He turned the notebook around and wrote it down. "Do you want to do research on the apartment leases or locations?"

I wasn't' sure what the location research would involve, but it sounded less boring than the leases. "I'll take locations." I remembered Ms. Ella's advice to write everything down. "I guess I should start by writing down the names of the neighborhoods on the New Orleans map Aly gave me and then find out about prices and safety."

Jax smiled for the first time since we left the castle. "Sounds like a plan. I'll use the crystal globe to read about leases."

While he went into the office, I pulled out the map and made a list of the neighborhoods. Château Magique was in City Circle, but the other places had names that sounded silly, and lots of them were named after food. Alligator Alley, Gumbo Gardens, Crawfish Court, Beignets Bayou, that kind of thing.

The map showed that the buildings along the blue river had little parks in between them, but the center of this New Orleans was all buildings and streets. The neighborhood called Turtle Town didn't have a single park. I wondered if there was even a tree. Closer to High Street, things were more spread out, but not much.

A few minutes later, Jax walked out of the office with a thick stack of paper. "You can use the globe. I printed what I need for now."

I wasn't sure how to find rentals on a crystal globe, but I wasn't going to tell him that. It was really just a round smartphone, wasn't it? Alligator Alley was between Turtle Town and Jackson Square, so I decided to start my search there. "Apartment rentals in Alligator Alley," I said, and a list appeared inside the clear crystal. "Scroll down." The list went on for dozens of pages, so I narrowed the search. "Show me small two-bedroom apartments in Alligator Alley." I didn't know what I was looking for, so I clicked on one just to see how much the rent was. It read:

2 Bedrooms, 1.5 baths, 658 square feet, AC
Laundry room: on site
Nearby: shopping, school, restaurants
$1,095 per month + $1,195 deposit/12-month lease

That's ridiculous!

I searched one-bedroom apartments to compare prices, but they weren't much cheaper.

There was no way I was living in Turtle Town, but I searched two-bedrooms there anyway, just to see how much they were. The cheapest ones were five hundred dollars a month and were in buildings that looked like warehouses—they didn't even have windows. And most of them didn't have elevators, either, so the higher floors were cheaper. But the ads for rentals in City Circle said the top floors were the most expensive. Maybe we could find something between Alligator Alley and Turtle Town.

Over the next couple hours, I searched too many apartments to count. Everything above Turtle Town cost twice as much. I was starting to feel discouraged. How much would we have to make to live someplace with windows? I decided to stop looking at apartments for a while and start making a list of jobs to apply for.

"Show me job listings for City Circle." What I really wanted was to work at a restaurant in the French Market so I could try all the food, but I didn't have any experience as a hostess or server and definitely wasn't qualified to work in the kitchen. As I was scrolling through the jobs listed, Jax came in.

"I found these menus on top of the fridge." He handed them to me. "They all deliver, but only until six."

"What time *is* it?"

“Sixty minutes until sunset,” the globe said. “Ninety minutes until curfew.”

“So there *is* a curfew,” Jax said, looking stupidly happy about being right.

“That’s not a good thing!” I stood up and looked out the window. “Why is there a curfew?”

“The rules change after dark,” the globe said.

“What does that mean?”

“It means you have one hour to receive a delivery.”

“I wonder why Ms. Ella didn’t tell us about the curfew,” Jax said.

“I don’t know, but I’m gonna starve to death if we don’t get some food.”

“There’s a kitchen full of food.”

“Those are ingredients. I want dinner.”

He rolled his eyes and handed me the menus. “Pick a place and figure out what you want.”

“Did you pick one?”

“No. They charge to deliver, so I’ll get something from the place you pick.”

Instead of being grateful, I was suspicious. Jax had been a jerk for as long as I’d known him. “And what do you get out of this deal?”

“I get to pick the restaurant next time. It’s called taking turns.”

I didn’t trust him, but the picture of crawfish gumbo had my name on it. Jax ordered a po’boy, and while we waited for dinner, we told each other what we’d learned so far from our research. We also agreed that we should list the highest-paying jobs we thought we could get. We figured the pay scale would be different here, but our lists would give us a place to start. After we both came up with six possible jobs, we shared our lists.

Zoe

Job	Pay per hour
Babysitter	$16
Pet sitter/dog walker	$15
Yard worker	$14
Receptionist	$13
Barista	$12
Ice cream scooper	$11

Jax

Job	Per Hour
Tutor	$20
Movie theater cashier	$15
Prep cook	$13
Lifeguard	$12
Barista	$12
Busboy	$10

"*Tutor*?" I said. "Get real." Jax wasn't exactly a star student.

"It's real," he said without looking up from his notebook.

"What subject?"

"What do you care?" This time he looked up and the expression on his face made it clear that he was dead serious. "Makes as much sense as you writin' down yard worker. What kind of yard work has your ass ever done?"

"I've done some." Raking leaves was about it, but how hard could it be? "Babysitting and dog walking probably pay best, but I don't think people will trust me if I can't give them names of some people I worked for."

"Maybe we should find out how much these jobs really pay and then we can make résumés for the ones that pay the most."

The chime rang, and I got up to answer the door.

"I'll get it," Jax said, sliding in front of me.

I handed him two twenties and a ten. "The ten's for the tip."

"That would be a 25 percent tip!" He handed the ten back to me. "Give me six bucks. That's 15 percent of forty dollars, which should be about right."

I handed him the cash and wondered why he was getting Cs in math.

The gumbo smelled amazing and so did Jax's sandwich. "Want to eat in the office so we can look up jobs and pay scales?" I was suddenly feeling more harmonious. Good food had a way of doing that.

He looked like he was considering it, but he said, "Let's sit at the table and enjoy it. We can work a couple more hours after we eat."

Having dinner with Jax at the long dining room table felt weirdly adult.

"Let's not talk business at dinner," Jax said.

That was fine by me, but I didn't know what else we could talk about. Even though we went to school together, the only things I knew about him were that he was a busboy at Santiago's, hung out at the boxing rink sometimes and was a sick skater.

He held up his glass. "Let's toast to being more successful than we ever dreamed we could be."

I held up my glass. "Including getting back home."

We clinked our glasses together and I felt like I was dreaming. And for all I knew, I *was* dreaming. Or maybe I was in a coma with a concussion or something, like Dorothy when the window frame hit her on the head and she woke up in Oz.

"Did you hear about the time Principal Snyder farted at graduation?" Jax said.

"He did not." Jax had a reputation for stretching the truth.

"He did. And it was so loud everybody in the whole auditorium started cracking up, and when he asked them to get quiet, people laughed harder."

"And then what?"

"He walked off the stage. Didn't even introduce the graduating class. The vice principal got up and did it."

"Mrs. Claiborne?"

"No, that was before she came to Garfield. But the teachers thought it was so funny that they bought a whoopee cushion and put it on his chair in the teachers' lounge."

I laughed. "Good to know some teachers have a sense of humor. The ones I have this year don't even smile."

When we'd both cleaned our plates, Jax carried them to the kitchen and came back with two wine glasses filled with peanut M&M's.

"Where'd you get *those*?"

"The vending machine in the lobby." He was smiling from ear to ear when he handed me my glass.

"Amazing!"

I devoured a green and red one and then let a yellow one melt in my mouth. Jax tossed an entire handful into his mouth, and we both got lost in our own worlds while we made the chocolate disappear—without magic.

In the quiet, I heard something clicking in the kitchen. "I think the ice machine might be stuck or something."

Jax listened and then put his finger in front of his lips and knelt down next to my chair.

“What is it?” I whispered.

“It’s tapping,” he said. “And it’s right outside the door.”

Nine

-△-

JAX

I was using the crystal globe to look for new places to post my tutoring flier and still couldn't believe what I was reading. There were colleges in Imagine, but no elementary or middle or high schools. We'd wondered why Ms. Ella hadn't said anything about us going to school but didn't want to bring it up. Kids from age seven to seventeen were in a program called Excel. They picked what they wanted to learn and got matched up with somebody who was good at it.

Incredible.

I scrolled down through the explanation and found out they didn't even use the words *teacher* or *tutor.* No wonder nobody was calling about my flier! It said anybody twelve or older could be a demonstrator, practitioner or expert, depending on how much experience or talent they said. It looked like I could be a demonstrator and get paid thirty bucks an hour. I was calculating how much I could make a week when Ms. Ella's face appeared.

"Good morning, Jax."

"Hey, Ms. Ella." I was worried we hadn't done a good enough job with the budget and the résumés we sent her and wished Zoe was back from her interview.

"I've received information from my informants about the clown." She frowned. "I'll wait until Zoe joins us so I only need to say it once."

"She's at an interview."

"Alone?"

"Um, well, yeah." *Should I have gone with her?* "The health club she's trying to get a job at is right across the street."

She closed her eyes and took a deep breath. "Please go wait for her outside the club and walk her home." Her face vanished as instantly as it had appeared.

Okay, jeez.

I was used to Ms. Ella being direct and all, but that seemed a little rude. And it made me a little nervous. What was she so uptight about?

I grabbed my key from the hook by the door and made sure it was locked before I called the elevator, which you did by waving your hand in front of the blue light between the two elevator doors.

Wait—what if we missed each other?

If I was going down when she was coming up, I'd be standing outside the club waiting like a dumb-ass while she was inside the apartment. I went back to the apartment to leave her a note and was unlocking the door when I heard the elevator bell. Just as I'd expected.

"I was just—"

But it wasn't Zoe getting off the elevator. It was the clown.

I darted back into the apartment and looked through the peephole. He was standing across from the elevator doors like he was waiting for—

Shit—is he waiting for Zoe? Did he recognize her somehow? Does he know she's living here?

I didn't know if I should keep an eye on the hallway or call Ms. Ella. The coalition couldn't come to New Orleans, but maybe she knew somebody close by who could help. But what if Zoe came back while I wasn't keeping an eye out for her?

Damn it.

The elevator chimed and I held on to the doorknob, ready to run out there if I had to. When a blue-skinned woman wearing a white tux and top hat stepped off the elevator with a white lion on a leash, though, I let go of the knob like it was on fire. They walked toward the clown, and when the lion roared at him, he backed up against the wall.

"May I see your ID, sir?" she said as she held up some kind of badge.

The clown's hands shook as he searched around in his jacket pockets, and he said something about misplacing his key, but she wasn't buying it. "I'll escort you from the building. And if I see you here again, it'll be an automatic thousand dollar fine." The elevator chimed. "After you."

The lion growled again and looked like it really wanted to snap its leash, and the clown tiptoed sideways to the elevator. I wouldn't have turned *my* back either.

I wrote Zoe a note telling her to stay put if she got home before me, and I was just about to leave when I heard a key in the door and she waltzed in. Literally. Or at least it was *one* of those kinds of ballroom dances.

"Guess who got a part in the Haunted Manor show!" She twirled around in a circle. "Meee!" It was still strange to see her with black hair and turquoise skin. "And guess how much it pays!"

"More than the job at the club, I hope."

She glided across the living room with her arms out like she was dancing with someone. "Twice as much!" Then she bowed.

"Get out! You're gonna make twenty dollars an hour to be in a show? Doing what?"

She laughed. "Doing this!" She danced by me again with her invisible partner. "They want to jack up the jump scares, so they're putting me in a ballroom scene with dancing ghosts. People will think I'm a ghost, and when I'm right in front of them, I'll point at them and scream my head off." She laughed again and flopped down on the couch.

"Congratulations." I didn't want to ruin her good mood by telling her about the clown, but Ms. Ella was going to tell her about it in a minute anyway. "Ms. Ella called. She said to call her back when you got home." I walked toward the office, and she rushed through the door ahead of me.

"I can't wait to tell her about my job!" She waved her hand and the crystal globe lit up. "Ms. Ella, please."

A few seconds later, Ms. Ella's face appeared. "Thank goodness you're safe."

"Safe from what?" Zoe said.

"The clown was spotted in City Circle." She paused like she was trying to figure out how much she wanted to tell us. "I received word that he was given a warning for trespassing and was escorted from the building."

Zoe's face faded from turquoise to mint green. "From *this* building? *When*?"

"A few minutes ago. I'm waiting to hear where he was when the guard found him."

I cleared my throat. "He was here." They both stared at me. "I was on my way to meet Zoe when I thought I'd better leave her a note in case I missed her. That's when the clown got out of the elevator and I ran inside to see what he'd do next."

"What *did* he do next?" Ms. Ella said.

"He leaned against the wall across from the elevators like he was waiting for somebody, and a couple minutes later a guard showed up with a lion."

"A lion!" Ms. Ella shook her head. "I'm afraid things are worse than I thought."

"Do you think he was after *me*?" Zoe said. "How could he even recognize me the way I look now?"

I was wondering the same things.

Ms. Ella pressed her lips together. "It's best not to speculate. When I receive a copy of the report, I'll talk to the mayor about having the clown detained for questioning. I'll also appoint bodyguards for both of you, starting tomorrow."

"What about tonight?" Zoe said, her color still looking more minty than turquoise.

"Stay inside with the door locked. The building manager will turn on iris recognition so only residents and registered guests will be able to get in."

We both nodded, and then Zoe couldn't hold it in anymore. "I got a job in the Haunted Manor show for twenty dollars an hour! Can the bodyguard go there with me?"

"I thought your interview was at the health club across the street," Ms. Ella said.

"Turns out Ms. DeVos owns the health club *and* the manor. When she saw my gymnastics routine, she asked if I had ballroom dance experience, and even though I've only seen it online, with my jazz and ribbon background I said I was sure I could learn the routine." She sounded mature all of a sudden.

Ms. Ella looked impressed. "And did Ms. DeVos ask to see your résumé?"

"No. She hired me right there on the spot," Zoe said, smiling proudly.

"Good. It needs work before you show it to anyone."

"But I already got a job. I don't need to fix my résumé now." Zoe's smile turned into a pout.

Ms. Ella raised her eyebrows. "One of the reasons I climbed the corporate ladder so quickly was that my résumé was always up to date and polished. When I'm hiring, I automatically reject candidates who have misspelled words and other mistakes on their résumés."

It sounded a little harsh to me, but I wasn't about to argue with her. Especially since I hadn't even scored an interview yet.

"Jax, please help Zoe to correct and update her résumé." She smiled. "Yours is perfect."

I didn't have to look at Zoe to know she was giving me the evil eye.

"Now, about your budget." The budget we'd sent her appeared on the big screen hanging over the office desk.

Monthly Budget

Income: .... $3,000 ($1,500 each)

Expenses:

Rent: $1,500
(Utilities included)

Groceries: $400

Loan Payment: $400

Total Expenses $2,300

Profit: .... $ 700
($350 each)

"Let's just say you're off to a decent start," Ms. Ella said.

I knew the math was right—what else did she want us to do?

"You didn't deduct New Orleans income tax. If you each make $18,000 a year, you'll owe about $2,000 for taxes, which is about $167 a month each."

I did the math in my head. That would only leave $366 a month for us to split, $183 each. "Ms. Ella, if there's money we don't spend, will we be able to take it back to L.A. with us?"

"Yes, and the exchange rate will be in your favor. But you'll both need to make more than $1,500 a month if you're going to have money left over."

"Why?" Zoe said, still looking bummed.

"In addition to leaving out income tax, you didn't include banking fees, you haven't budgeted anything to create a three-month emergency cushion, and you've budgeted too much for rent."

"But the only places for less than $1,500 are in Turtle Town," Zoe whined. "They're in warehouses, and some don't even have windows."

"Most financial experts say you shouldn't spend more than 30 percent of your income for housing. That means if you make $3,000, you shouldn't spend more than $900 a month on rent." She tapped her pen on her notebook. "You either have to gross an extra $2,000 a month or get used to living without windows."

"By gross, do you mean what we have left after all the taxes and expenses?"

She shook her head. "No. Gross income is how much you make, total, and net income is what you have left after expenses. It's what you called profit."

My head started spinning. If we had to spend this much money, I wouldn't have any money to help my mom when I got back. Talking about our annual income made it feel like we were never going to get home. "Do you know how much health insurance will be for us?"

"What's health insurance?"

Zoe reached for the "What We Know About Imagine" notebook.

After I explained what it was, Ms. Ella looked like I'd just told her she was fat. "You're saying you have to pay for health care, and if you don't use the money you pay to the insurance company, you don't get it back?"

"Not just that," Zoe said, "but the insurance usually doesn't even cover the whole bill."

Ms. Ella narrowed her eyebrows like she was trying to figure out if we were messin' with her.

"It's true," I said.

"That might be the most ridiculous thing I've ever heard." She shook her head. "No health insurance here. If you're sick or you get hurt, the healers take care of you until you're better."

"So if we don't have to pay for that stuff, why do we need to have an emergency cushion for three months?" Zoe said. "We don't even know if we'll be here that long."

"That's right. That's precisely what saving and preparing for the unexpected means. None of us knows what tomorrow will bring." The message light in the corner of her screen started blinking. "It's City Circle security. I need to take this. Please submit your revised budget tomorrow." And then she was gone.

If Ms. Ella hadn't said for us to stay put for the rest of the day, I'd have gone out and posted new math demonstrator flyers. But I was stuck here with pouting Zoe, who obviously needed an attitude adjustment.

"At least you got a job," I said. "How about if I fix your résumé while you make supper and then we can do the budget over again?"

She dragged herself to the door like her feet were too heavy to lift. "Macaroni and cheese it is."

"Spaghetti is on today's menu."

"But I don't know how to make that." She was whining again.

We'd been here a week, and so far she hadn't made any of the meals we planned. She was using up our lunch supply instead of cooking. "I bought everything we need and put the recipe on the counter. Just follow the directions."

I was expecting a smart-ass remark, so I was surprised when she started to cry. "C'mon, Zoe, it's not that bad. Aren't you tired of canned soup and mac and cheese?"

That just made her cry harder, and I had no idea what to do.

Ten

-∇-

ZOE

I walked back to the *X* that marked my starting position in the middle of the ballroom and waited for my cue. After dancing to the same minute of *The Sleeping Beauty Waltz* for six days, it was stuck in my head.

My earphone buzzed and the voice said, "Five, six, seven, eight." I lifted up my arms to join my ghost partner, who would appear when the music started.

"Hello, Mr. Bones," I said when he appeared. I called him that because his "skin" was kind of see-through, so he looked like a mix of a ghost and a skeleton. He was a few inches taller than me and had a nice smile, but his eyes were spooky, so I usually looked over his shoulder instead of right at him.

Coordinating my steps with his, I made sure our hands were "touching" as we moved around the other waltzing ghost couples.

As bored as I was with the music, I wasn't tired of the ballroom. The floor was green marble and the high ceiling was painted sky blue with puffy clouds. At least as tall as me, the rotating chandeliers made dancing rainbows on the white walls. I thought it would be amazing to go to a real ball here and wondered if Ms. DeVos ever hosted parties.

Mr. Bones took me for a second spin around the dance floor, and when we stopped at the designated spot in front of the train full of people, I turned toward them and screamed for the last time today. Some of them screamed back, and the stage rotated to the haunted library set. *Gracias a dios. (Thank God.)*

I left the ballroom through the hidden door behind the tapestry of Versailles and followed the narrow hallway to the dressing room. The dancer who had the next shift was just leaving. I couldn't tell if the girls who worked before and after me were people or animatrons, but I stopped saying hi to them because they looked right through me. Rude, but then, most animatrons weren't programmed with good manners. If they were real girls, that kind of sucked, but it wasn't like I was trying to make friends here.

Normally, I'd hang my gown in the wardrobe room, but I had tomorrow off and had to pick up my check and drop my costume off at the laundry room. So instead of taking the tunnel to the staff exit, I took the employee stairway to the first floor and hoped my bodyguard Slash remembered to meet me out front today. Even though the coalition had their informants on the lookout, nobody had seen the clown since the guard caught him in our apartment building.

As I approached the first-floor door, there was a circle on the floor that said "Stop Here." The screen in the door flashed, taking my photo, and a few seconds later the door slid open. I was relieved that the system recognized me because Jax said facial recognition didn't always work. The long hallway in front of me was bright, but as I walked toward the office at the other end, the people in the paintings staring down at me gave me the creeps. Hearing my footsteps echoing didn't help either. I was starting to wonder if *real* ghosts lived here. Next payday, I'd wear my Vans instead of my sandals so I didn't call so much attention to myself.

The manor took up a whole city block, and I passed dozens of closed doors on my way down the hall. Some of them had fancy nameplates, and others had warning signs like "Stay Out!" and "Don't Even Think About It." One said, "I'd Turn Back If I Were You," and it made me think of the wicked witch in *The Wizard of Oz*. The hair on my arms stood up as I hurried past the door.

I was wondering if I was the only person here when a little boy walked out of a door in front of me. He headed down the hall the same way I was going, and when I passed the door he'd come through, I saw that the sign on it read, "Shortcut."

It turned out we were both going to the office, and I walked in after him and signed my name on the electronic clipboard. In the waiting room, there were two white leather chairs that looked like nobody ever sat in them, so I leaned against the wall to wait for someone to show up with my check. Although we were the only two people there, the boy didn't seem any more interested in talking to me than I was in talking to him, so we both stared at the floor. But out of the corner of my eye, I could see that his face was dirty and his nose was red. He couldn't have been more than five or six years old, and I wondered why he wasn't with an adult. He looked human except for his eyes, which looked like a cat's, but there were tons of people in New Orleans who didn't look like the people at home. Including me now.

A week ago, I had my heart set on celebrating my first check at Mr. Ed's Oyster Bar & Fish House, but Jax killed that dream when he showed me how the math worked out. We had to follow the rule of paying ourselves first, which wasn't as good as it sounds. It meant we had to put 10 percent of every check in a high-yield savings account and make ends meet with 90 percent of our income. So the first $48 of my $480 paycheck was for that, and after I took out the money for taxes, plus my share of the groceries and the other expenses, I'd only have $16 left.

I jumped when the buzzer rang, and I looked up to see a tall man with silver skin and long black hair walk into the waiting room carrying a shiny black tray with two white envelopes on it. "Mistress Zoe" was typed on one, and the other said "Master H."

"Thanks," I said as I put mine in the zipper compartment of my backpack.

Then the man lowered the tray so the boy could reach the other one. "Take this right to the master," the man said in a voice that sounded like it was coming from a deep cave.

The boy snatched the envelope with a furry paw and darted out the door. *Cat eyes* and *paws?*

As the silver guy turned to go back into the office, I remembered that I didn't know where the laundry room was. "Sir, can you please tell me how to get to laundry room?"

"What laundry room?"

"Um, the one where I'm supposed to take my costume."

"If you take the shortcut, you will arrive before it's too late. But I don't recommend it."

Too late for what? "Well, which way *do* you recommend?"

"I can't say that I recommend any of the ways." He pulled out a pocket watch and frowned at it.

"Is it about to close or something?"

He held out his hand. "I'll take it." He folded it over his arm and looked down at me. "The front door will be locking in a few minutes. I'd hurry if I were you."

Didn't have to tell *me* twice. I sprinted down the hall to the glass exit doors and was relieved to see Slash next to one of the lion statues, standing so still he looked like a statue himself. "Hey, Slash," I said as I stepped outside.

He looked up and smiled. "How's it feel to get your first paycheck?"

"Pretty good." I didn't feel right about complaining. "I have to go to the grocery store, but we can go home for lunch first if you're hungry."

He handed me a paper bag. "Not the healthiest, but we need to get over to the castle. You can eat 'em on the way."

"The castle?" I opened the bag, and there were a half dozen round, puffy pastries dusted with powdered sugar. "Beignets! This is amazing. I've been wanting to try these since we got here." I took a bite of one and let the sugar melt in my mouth before I chewed it. *Dios mío. (My God.)* I stared at the golden interior.

Slash waved a hand in front of me. "Uh, Zoe?"

"Oh . . . sorry. Right," I said with my mouth half full. "Why do we have to go to the castle? Our meeting was supposed to be tomorrow."

He waved his hand to hail a carriage. "There's been a development."

The driverless carriage, pulled by red plaid animatron horses, stopped and we climbed up onto the seat.

"Does Jax know?"

"He's already there."

As we went, I devoured three beignets and was reaching for a fourth when it occurred to me that I should probably save some for Jax, so I folded the top of the bag and ignored the temptation to eat number four.

The human-driven carriages could easily take ten minutes to get from uptown New Orleans to the southern exit to High Street, but the animatrons' sensors made it easier for them to weave through the crowded streets, and we got there in half the time.

I didn't need a guard inside the castle, so Slash could have some time to himself while I was in the meeting. It was a short walk up the steps to the front door, but the magic entrance through the mosaic carriage was faster and more fun. "I want to take the shortcut. Can you snap for me?"

"Still don't have it down, huh?" The twinkle in his eyes said he was just teasing me, but I still felt embarrassed.

When he snapped his fingers, the two-dimensional carriage became three-dimensional.

"I'll meet you back here in an hour."

"Okay. Thanks again for the beignets."

The door opened and I climbed in. As I slid on the seat to the opposite door, the word *shortcut* echoed in my head, and I wondered why the silver guy didn't recommend taking the shortcut to the laundry room. *The cat boy came out of that door, so how bad could it be?*

I knew better than to run in Ms. Ella's castle, so I speed-walked down the hall of trees, keeping a sharp eye out for animatrons. The bruise on my right arm reminded me that collisions were a lot harder on me than they were on them. Her lab door was open, and Fibonacci and Fermat said hi when I walked in.

I expected to round the bookcases and see Jax and Ms. Ella at the table where we'd had dinner, but instead they were sitting on swings hanging from the ceiling by purple ropes. Ms. Ella was facing the sunflowers and Jax was facing the other direction.

"Hi, Ms. Ella. Hey, Jax." I tossed him the bag of beignets. "Hi, Aly." She was standing on the swing on the other side of Jax, facing the same way as Ms. Ella.

Aly said hi and sniffed the air. "Do I smell beignets?"

"Yep. Slash bought 'em for me to celebrate my first paycheck. There's three left."

Jax held up the bag to Aly and Ms. Ella and looked relieved when they said no.

Ms. Ella pointed to the empty swing next to her. "Have a seat, Zoe. Face the same direction as Jax so I can see you two while we're swinging."

"Um, okay."

"I'm a firm believer that swinging makes bad news go down easier." She smiled. "Sort of like a spoonful of sugar, but it won't rot your teeth or ruin your figure."

I'd already guessed the news was bad, but hearing her say it still made my mouth go dry. Jax put his beignet back in the bag and set it on the floor.

The swings started without even needing a push, and when we were swinging so high that we could almost touch the glass ceiling with our toes, Aly finally sat down on the seat.

Whew. She'd been making me nervous.

As we swung, I understood why Ms. Ella wanted us to face in opposite directions—the swings were timed so that Jax and I always faced her and Aly until we passed them at the bottom, and then again after we passed them going backward.

Clever, but what is all this leading up to?

Every time we swung toward them, I expected Ms. Ella to say something, but she didn't.

Please, let's get this over with.

If we'd been sitting on chairs, every minute of waiting would have made my stomach get tighter, but strangely enough, it was just the opposite on the swings. I could feel myself relaxing. I should have known—Ms. Ella had a reason for everything she did. Nothing was just a coincidence.

Finally, she broke the silence. "We have reason to believe there are animatrons that are nearly identical to the clown in question." Our swings passed and she waited until we were facing each other again to continue. "After not seeing him for a week, several of our informants saw him in different sectors of New Orleans at the same time."

The swings slowed down but kept going just as high. It felt more like floating than swinging.

"One of them was seen going in the back door of the DeVos Manor," Aly said.

A chill ran through me like a river of ice water.

"We don't know how many there are," Ms. Ella said, "but we suspect that they all answer to the human clown who threatened Zoe."

Deep breaths.

"We've also learned that the human clown comes from a long line of dancing clowns. They call him Master Hoofer."

I gasped. *The name on the envelope.*

"Maybe this is a coincidence," I said as I swung toward Ms. Ella, "but when I got my check, a boy with cat eyes and paws picked up an envelope for Master H."

The swings slowed down further and only went half as high.

"Tell me every single thing that happened today," Ms. Ella said.

I told her everything I could remember, and when I got to the part about what the silver guy said about the shortcut and the laundry room, I noticed that she and Aly gave each other a look. Then Jax and I gave each other a look.

After a few minutes of silence that had me in suspense all over again, Aly said, "Who told you to take your costume to the laundry room?"

"Ms. DeVos. There was a note on the dressing room bulletin board from her."

"How do you know it was from her?" Ms. Ella said.

"She signed it. And it was on her stationery."

"Hold on," Ms. Ella said, and the swings slowed to a stop. "Zoe, we happen to know that Ms. DeVos took the shuttle to a nearby dimension two days ago. I think somebody else wrote that note and forged her signature."

"By 'somebody else,' do you mean the clown?" Jax said.

She didn't answer. I had questions too, but my mouth was too dry to say anything.

"Unfortunately," Ms. Ella said, "the multiple clowns and forged note are not all that we learned of today. We found evidence that kids aren't playing avatars from home. Master Hoofer and his gang kidnap them and turn them into avatars for the game." She locked eyes with me. "The boy with cat eyes and paws is probably in transition."

If my feet hadn't been on the ground, I would have fallen off the swing.

"And that's not all." She got off her swing and stood in front of me. "We think the kids are being held at the manor. We need you to help us find out where."

"Me?" I somehow managed to squeak out. "I couldn't even find the laundry room."

Aly got off her swing and stood next to her. "There is no laundry room in that building. The costumes are picked up in the dressing room and sent to the dry cleaner across the road. Somebody was trying to trick you into taking the shortcut or staying in the building after the doors were locked."

Now Jax stood up. Apparently, I was the only one whose legs had stopped working. "They figured she'd get locked in while she was looking for a room that wasn't there?"

"That's what it looks like," Ms. Ella said.

I slid my feet back and forth on the floor, trying to get some strength back into my legs. "But Slash can't go inside the manor with me. I want to help, but what chance do I have against a bunch of evil clowns?"

"Gotta say it sounds like a suicide mission," Jax said.

Fibonacci and Fermat gasped.

Ms. Ella glared at Jax. "I'll pretend you didn't say that." She turned back to me. "We'll have one of our senior guards in every audience during your shift. And after your last shift, they'll escort you to the back door where Slash and Burns, your new guard, will be waiting. They'll be with you everywhere you go."

"What about in between shifts, when I'm looking for the kids?"

"That part you'll have to do on your own. But since you work there, if a guard finds you in a section of the manor you don't have clearance for, you can say you don't know the best way to the exit and ask them to show you. Since you don't know the full layout of the manor, you won't be lying."

I'm not gonna lie. I was terrified of that clown, and knowing there were a bunch of them made me want to cry. But I couldn't stop thinking about the kids I saw in that hallway and how scared they were.

Ms. Ella put her hands on my shoulders, and suddenly strength seemed to flow into my body and all the way down to my toes. When I stood up, my legs were steady and I wasn't even that scared. I swallowed the lump in my throat and found my voice.

"I don't know if I can do it, but I know I have to try."

Eleven

-△-

JAX

I checked my reflection in the restroom mirror to make sure I looked okay. The black pants and tan button-down shirt Ms. Ella had given me looked all right, and the shoes were real leather, but it was the sport coat that pulled it all together. Zoe saw it on a sales rack on her way home from work and talked me into buying it for my first math demonstrator interview. She even loaned me the money. She was probably tired of being the only one working.

I reached for my phone to check the time, but then I remembered for the thousandth freakin' time that I didn't have one. Nobody here did. Sure, they had animatrons, magic and crystal ball Internet, but smart phones and cell phones? Forget it. So I walked back to the lobby to find out how much time I had till the interview. It would only take a few minutes to get to the grill, but

I'd give myself twice that long in case something unexpected came up—Ms. Ella was always pounding that habit into our heads like a jackhammer.

The grandfather clock said I had fifteen minutes, so I went into the Pro Shop to burn some time. They had all the regular golf stuff—clubs, umbrellas, shoes, gloves, clothes—but my eye went past all that to the picture of Aly on the wall behind the cash register. She was holding a trophy, and Ms. Ella and Arthur were standing next to her.

They said they couldn't come to New Orleans. I'd definitely be asking them about that.

The clock, shaped like a golf ball, said it was five till one, so I headed over to the Mirage Grill. When I got to the podium outside, two people were in line ahead of me, so I had a minute to check out the hostess. She was about my age, with big blue eyes and long purple hair, and she looked like she spent a lot of time working out. Definitely the hottest girl I'd seen since we got here. If I wasn't there for an interview, I'd have laid down some bars. But I just went with "I'm Jax. I'm meeting Mr. Redla."

"Hi, Jax." Her engraved nametag said "Cheyenne," and her smile was so bright she could have starred in a toothpaste commercial. "Mr. Redla decided to get lunch to go. He'd like you to meet him outside."

"Oh, okay. Thanks, Cheyenne."

"Sure. You can call me Chey."

"Chey." I wish I'd had more time to hit her up, but after waiting two weeks to get an interview, I couldn't be late. The hallway to the lobby was filled with golfers heading to the restaurant, so I had to swim upstream to make it to the front door. When I stepped outside I saw a man in shorts and a golf shirt who looked like the guy I read about on the globe. But he looked different without his suit.

"Mr. Redla?"

"Well, hello. You must be Jax."

"Yes, sir." I extended my right hand. "Nice to meet you."

"Likewise." He had a toothpaste smile, too. "Isn't this a beautiful day?"

"Yes, sir." The green grass and the purple sky looked like a painting. Imagine's sky was different colors on different days, and nobody seemed to know why.

"How'd you like to do the interview on the golf course? If you're up for caddying nine holes, there's a hundred bucks in it for you."

I wasn't sure. I knew what caddies did, but I'd never done it.

"It's okay if you don't have experience. All you need to do is carry my clubs and calculate the distances. It'll give you a chance to impress me with your math skills."

I knew I had to do it, but I couldn't walk across a golf course in these shoes and clothes. How was I going to make this happen? Then I remembered that the Pro Shop had everything I needed. "Yeah, uh, I just need a minute to get changed." Before he could say anything, I bolted back into the clubhouse. We'd been approved for a credit card with a $3,000 spending limit, and I used it to buy shoes, socks, shorts and the cheapest short sleeve shirt I could find. It came to $175, but I could take my time paying it off, so I wasn't worried about it. A few minutes later, I was back outside wearing my new clothes and carrying the old ones in a Pro Shop shopping bag.

Mr. Redla was at a patio table under a big umbrella. "That was fast." He smiled and slid a boxed lunch across the table. "I hope you like oysters."

"Thanks." Inside was a po'boy with a side of slaw and the biggest strawberries I'd ever seen. There was a pitcher of ice water on the table, and I filled my glass. After I set the pitcher back down, I wondered if I should have offered to fill his glass, too. *Uh-oh.*

While we ate, he asked about my favorite subjects, what sports I liked, if I had any hobbies and what kind of job experience I had. I was worried about telling him I was from another dimension and couldn't get myself to say that word, so I just said I was from Los Angeles and he didn't seem to have a problem with it. He didn't even ask how long I was planning to stay. I knew lunch was part of the interview, but he made it feel like just a couple dudes sitting around choppin' it up, so I started to chill. I could have powered through the po'boy in seconds, but I forced myself to take small bites so I could answer his questions without making him wait forever for me to chew. I'd learned that I was supposed to have some good questions ready to ask him, too, so the next time *he* took a bite, I asked him how old he was when he knew he wanted to be a lawyer and how he started his law business.

"Just about *your* age" he said, and then he told me how he got started and how he grew his firm into a multimillion-dollar firm. It was a great story, and now that he was doing most of the talking, I had a chance to actually eat my lunch. The po'boy and strawberries were killer, but the coleslaw was a little flat, so I added some pepper.

"Did you learn to taste food before seasoning it at Santiago's?" he asked.

"Chef Liza would cut off my hand with her cleaver if she saw me add seasoning to something she made," I said. "It was my mom who taught me to taste food before adding salt or pepper to it." I didn't tell him it was because we used free packets from fast food restaurants to save a few bucks. Thinking about her made my throat tighten up a little, and I was glad to see a kid in a country club uniform walking up to our table.

"Good afternoon, Mr. Redla. May I offer you a ride to the side nine?"

The side *nine? Never heard that before.*

"Sure," he said, and then he noticed my shopping bag. "Do you want to put that in my locker?"

Carrying a bag of clubs and my own stuff would have been pretty awkward. "That would be great. Thanks."

He called over another one of the kids wearing country club uniforms. "Nigel, please give this to my daughter and ask her to put it in my locker."

I gave the kid my bag, hoping I could trust him, and Mr. Redla nodded toward the cart that was waiting for us. "Ready?"

"Yep." We climbed into the backseat, and the kid driving steered onto the cart path. I was happy to be outside, especially since I didn't need a bodyguard anymore. I got my freedom back yesterday because the coalition figured out that the clown was after Zoe.

"What do you think of our course?" Mr. Redla said.

"It's the nicest course I've ever been on." Actually, it was the *only* course I'd ever been on. It *was* nice, though, with palm trees and ponds and some long-legged birds I'd never seen before.

After another few minutes, the cart stopped at a stone archway. A black dog the size of a Hummer—literally—was lying on the other side. Mr. Redla got out like there was nothing to be afraid of.

"Uh, is that an animatron?"

"I wish," he said. "We'd save a boatload of money on food if he were."

"I didn't know dogs could get that big."

"He's a mix of black Lab, brown Lab, and Ms. Ella's lab."

"You know Ms. Ella?"

"Who doesn't?"

"I didn't know she was famous." The dog lifted his head and sniffed the air. "Is he friendly?"

"Major, show Jax here that you're friendly."

The dog stood up and wagged his tail. He could have eaten both of us in one bite.

Mr. Redla thanked the kid who drove the cart and asked him to pick us up at the ninth hole in a couple hours.

I forced myself to get out of the cart, but I almost dove back in when Major barked.

Mr. Redla laughed. "No need to worry, son. Major won't hurt you. He's just saying hello."

Yeah, right. I threw his golf bag over my shoulder and followed him through the archway. Major took a few steps back and stood in front of the tee box.

"We call this the side nine because it's not straightforward. It has obstacles, like Major's tail. You have to hit the ball through his legs without hitting him."

"For real? What if somebody hits him?"

He held up a golf ball-size whiffle ball. "We use this for the first hole. Once we get past Major, I'll switch to a regular ball." He walked over to the tee. "Every hole has two obstacles—one at the tee and one at the cup."

"Are they all alive?"

"In one way or another."

I had no idea what *that* meant, but I'd find out soon enough. I looked past Major and didn't see anyone else on the fairway. "Are we the only ones here?" I was starting to wonder if this had been a bad idea.

"We might be." He pulled a club out of the bag. "Most folks play the front and back nine. Not everybody likes to mix problem-solving with pleasure."

He took the cover off the club and it looked like a shovel.

What the . . .

"Major's legs are only fifteen feet long, so I can't use a club that's going to send the ball high into the air." He took a couple practice swings. "With this spade, I can hit the ball straight through Major's legs—that is, if he cooperates and keeps his tail out of the way."

I put the ball on the tee and Major sat down, completely blocking the way. "Doesn't look like he feels like cooperating."

Mr. Redla laughed. "That's what makes the side nine so interesting." He turned to the dog. "You're making me look bad in front of our guest."

Major whined and beat his tail on the ground, but he didn't stand up.

"Any idea what he might want?" Mr. Redla said while he took practice swings with the "spade."

"Maybe a dog biscuit or something?"

Major barked twice.

"I'm not falling for that." Mr. Redla pointed the spade at a pile of bones that looked like they came from dinosaurs. "You have plenty of bones."

"Maybe he wants us to pet him." As soon as the words were out of my mouth, I wished I could suck them back in. The dog whined again and lay down in front of me, stretching out so his massive paws were only a few feet away.

Holy . . .

"I think he likes you."

Uh-huh. "You sure this guy won't bite me?"

"Major, do you promise you won't bite Jax?"

Major nodded his head. For real. "Okay, Major, I'm gonna pet you, buddy. Do you like to have your head scratched?" He lowered his head to the ground and I could just barely reach the top of it. His fur was long and shaggy and felt like the fake fur blanket on Ms. Ella's lounge chair. "How's that, buddy?"

He yipped and slowly got on his feet. My heart was pounding so hard I swear I could hear it, but at least I passed the first test.

"Well done, Jax." He stepped up to the tee. "Good dog, Major!"

Major stood as still as a statue, holding his tail to one side, and Mr. Redla smacked the ball with the spade and sent it straight through the dog's legs. It went farther than I'd have expected and landed right in the middle of the fairway. "Nice!"

He slid his club back into the bag and we walked to the ball. "This hole is 333 yards. If you look at the closest sprinkler head, you can figure out how many yards from here to the cup."

The sprinkler heads looked like shrunken human heads with holes where the mouth, nose and eyes were. "This one says 44 yards, so 289 to go."

"That was some fast math."

It was actually easy, so I just nodded. "What club do you want for this one?"

"Let's go with the five wood. It has the purple sock on it."

I took the sock off and handed him the club, which looked like it had never been used.

"It's my lucky club." This time he didn't even take a practice swing. He just walked up to the tee, straightened his shoulders and sent the ball flying like a pro.

"Whoa! That was incredible." This dude could *golf.*

He handed the club back to me. "We'll see."

We passed a couple sand traps and then a big pond.

"Keep an eye on the edge of the pond. The gators are big and fast."

"*Alligators*?" I scanned the surface of the water and didn't see anything, but that didn't make me feel any better. "How often do you see 'em?"

"Not too often in the afternoon. They get fed at noon, so they're probably not hungry again yet."

Probably? I didn't want to sound scared, but this was a little wack. "What do we do if one comes after us?"

"Chances are that won't happen. But if it does"—he pulled a gold ball the size of a marble out his pocket—"I roll this toward it and we keep walking. Gators can't resist these. But if you run, instinct will take over, and trust me when I say you can't outrun a gator."

"I trust you." Damn right I trusted him.

He put the ball back in his pocket.

"So why can't they resist it? What *is* it?" I noticed I was walking faster than him and slowed down.

"It's a bella ball. *Bella* is Spanish for 'beautiful.'"

I was listening, but I wasn't following.

"When a gator sees its reflection in the gold, it's so taken by its own beauty that it can't look away and eventually falls asleep."

Come on. "Really?"

He laughed. "Beauty *is* in the eye of the beholder."

When we walked around the bend in the fairway, there was a giant doghouse, which I guess made sense, but I couldn't see how a ball was going to get through the house. As far as I could see, there were no holes in it.

It had a door that was big enough for Major, but it looked like a solid mirror. When we were a few yards away, the mirror made us both look a couple feet taller. “Cool! A convex mirror.”

“Is that what that thing’s called?” He was moving the clubs around in his bag like he was looking for something.

“The ones that make you look taller are convex. The ones that make you look shorter or fatter are concave.”

“Is that so?”

I hoped I didn’t sound like I thought I was all that. “I only know that because it was on a test last year.”

“Now where did I put that?” He fished around in the front pocket of his bag and pulled out a plastic compact. “Here it is.” He popped it open and held it up so I could see inside. “It’s a magnifying mirror.” He turned his back to the mirror on the doghouse and held the magnifying mirror over his shoulder. “Watch this.” He turned the mirror in his hand until it caught the sunlight, and when the light from the tiny mirror hit the mirror door, the door slid open.

“Whoa. How’d you figure *that* out?”

“I wish I could take all the credit.” He pulled his putter out of the bag and I set the ball on the tee in front of the open doghouse door. “My daughter was caddying for me, and while she was waiting for me to decide how I was going to hit around the doghouse, she put on some lip gloss and the mirror opened. Neither one of us knew how it happened, but I was determined to figure it out. Took a while, but it was worth it.” He gave the ball a solid smack and it sailed right through the opening, hit the bull’s-eye on the back wall and dropped into the hole. The electronic sign over the door flashed "EAGLE!!!" He was grinning from ear to ear. "And that's how it's done."

"How many people know the trick?"

He handed me the putter and I put it back in the bag. "Used to be two, now it's three. But it's just one of the tricks that will open the door. Every obstacle can be surmounted in at least four different ways."

I picked up his bag and followed the arrow that pointed to the next hole, wondering what sort of obstacle it would be this time. "How many times have you played the, uh, side nine?"

"Hundreds, and I still haven't figured out how to sink a putt in the ninth hole."

After a few more holes, I wondered how anybody could figure out any of the obstacles.

The sixth tee was at the entrance to a tunnel with a maze inside, and the maze walls could shift, so there was no guarantee a golfer would ever find his way out. Mr. Redla didn't explain this to me until we were already inside.

"But there's no reason for concern. Our engineers installed escape acoustics. All you have to do is snap your fingers and the maze will adjust to let you out the closest door."

It only took him a few minutes to find his way to the exit, but it felt like longer. Snap escapes or not, I was glad to be back outside.

Not that there was really any safe place on this "side nine." The putting green was surrounded by sand, and Mr. Redla warned me not to step on it. "It's quicksand. It's only a few feet deep, but we'd have to call a crew to shovel you out."

This is gettin' old. "So how do we get to the green?"

“We don’t. I have to chip it from here. If it goes in, it’ll come out of a slot at the next hole. If it doesn’t, the ball collector will grab it at the end of the day.”

He used his lucky club and put the ball right in the cup. It didn’t even hit the green.

Number seven was a small volcano.

“If I hit the ball into the hole, the eruption will shoot it all the way to the putting green.”

This time he missed and the ball rolled back down the small mountain and onto the fairway. It only took him two strokes to get to the hole, which was a giant lily pad floating on a pool shaped like an infinity symbol. We had to jump onto the pad without falling into the water because it was filled with jellyfish. No pressure.

At the eighth hole, there was a bakery made out of Legos that was owned and operated by gorillas who spoke English, Spanish and French. This was all actually starting to seem normal to me. To get their permission to tee off, we had to solve a riddle written on a chalkboard along with the day’s specials:

As I was going down the lane,
I met a man who was doing the same;
He tipped his hat an’ drew his cane,
And in this riddle I’ve told you his name.

I think I could have figured it out, but I didn’t have to because I already knew the answer. During COVID, a riddle like this was all over the Internet. “His name is Andrew.”

The gorillas clapped and Mr. Redla patted me on the back. “Bravo, Jax.”

I wanted to take all the credit, but he’d been straight with *me* about his daughter helping him figure out the first hole. “Thanks, but I heard a riddle a lot like this one before.”

He nodded and gave me a look that made me think I made the right choice by telling him.

When we made it to the hole, it was on the side of a giant loaf of rising bread. He bogeyed this hole and I wondered if he'd be pissed, but he just shrugged and handed me his club and started walking toward the last tee.

"I used to get upset about missing, but that takes the fun out of the game. Especially on the side nine. For me, the fun part is being rewarded for coming up with clever solutions and taking smart risks. You know the saying, Jax. You miss 100 percent of the shots you don't take."

"That makes sense, but how do you know about Michael Jordan?"

He stopped walking and looked at me. "Seriously?"

I suddenly wished I hadn't asked, but Zoe and I had been trying to figure out how much of our world this one knew about. "I know you know some things about Earth, but not which things."

"Would being able to figure it out help you to reach the goals you told me about setting?" he said.

"I don't know. Probably not."

"Then I wouldn't waste time thinking about it."

We rounded a dogleg on the fairway and the ninth hole came into view. It looked like a miniature version of Ms. Ella's castle, and the moat was filled with mermaids.

"What the heck?" Mr. Redla said.

They waved at us and one with bright red hair said, "That fella looks like the one who was walking with Zoe." They all looked at me.

"Hey, handsome," another said, "tell Zoe we've been waiting for her."

They all giggled and Mr. Redla looked at me with the most serious expression I'd seen on his face all day. "Don't say your name or mine." He turned to the mermaids. "Why aren't you in Riskville?"

"We were bored," they all said at the same time.

"Where are the dancing clowns?"

"We gave them the afternoon off," the redhead said.

"*You* gave them the afternoon off?"

I couldn't tell if he thought it was funny or if he was pissed off or both.

"When did you become managers of my club?"

Your club?

They giggled again, and the redhead said, "We just want to have fun. Don't be such a club in the mud."

They burst out laughing, like that was the funniest thing they'd ever heard, and Mr. Redla waited for them to stop. "Sorry, ladies, but if you're not gone by the time my security team arrives, you'll be cited for trespassing." Instead of trying to tee off, he walked across the drawbridge and I followed. "No point in taking the risk of slipping up around mermaids. I'll show you how this hole works another time."

I liked the sound of *another time.* "That would be great. Seeing the side nine definitely wasn't anything like what I was expecting."

"I'm glad you can appreciate it. The other kids I interviewed didn't make it past Major."

The inside of this castle was just one hallway with no door, and when we reached the other end, he pressed a call button for the cart before we went back outside. In less than a minute, the guy who dropped us off showed up, and I put Mr. Redla's bag in the back and got in. I wanted to know if he was going to hire me, but

I wasn't sure how to find out without asking him straight out. "So, uh, what kind of math does your daughter want to learn?"

"To tell you the truth, she's not sure she wants to learn more math. She thinks a calculator is all she needs. Her mom and I want her to develop an appreciation for math, but she doesn't have to take it for her next subject if she doesn't want to. Do you think you can show her that math is actually interesting and helpful?"

"I don't know, but I'll try. Being good at math helps me in lots of ways."

He took a business card out of his wallet and wrote his address on the back. "When can you start?"

"How about tonight?" The sooner I started making money, the better.

He smiled. "I like your enthusiasm. Unfortunately, we have a fundraiser tonight. How about tomorrow morning at nine?"

"That'll work." I put the card in my pocket, and a few minutes later the driver parked in front of the clubhouse and I hopped out and grabbed his bag. "Should I follow you to your locker?"

"Thanks, but I can take it from here." He handed me a Benjamin and I tried not to act like I'd never gotten one before.

"Thank you." As I put the bill in my pocket, a brown bear jogged up the sidewalk toward us on his hind legs. He was wearing a country club visor and a security badge. After the side nine, I wasn't sure anything was ever going to surprise me again.

"Afternoon, Mr. Redla. We got the call about the mermaid intrusion and headed right over, but they were gone when we got there."

"Do you know how they got in?"

"We're looking into it, sir. We think they might have picked the lock in the river gate between Riskville and Orleans."

"Okay. Let me know what you find out."

I was about to remind Mr. Redla that my bag was in his locker when Chey walked down the front steps carrying it. "Ready to go, Dad?"

Dad?

"I'd *better* be ready. We were supposed to be home thirty minutes ago." He took the golf bag I was holding. "Jax, this is my daughter. Cheyenne, say hi to the guy I hope will inspire you to learn math. He's coming over tomorrow."

"I told him to call me Chey."

"You two already know each other?"

"We met inside," she said.

"Hi, Chey."

She smiled and handed me my bag. "See you tomorrow."

"Thanks again, Jax," Mr. Redla said. "If you happen to see any of my clowns on your way home, tell 'em I didn't give them the afternoon off."

"Yes, sir." We shook hands again and I watched them walk into the parking lot, hoping like hell that I didn't see any dancing clowns on my way home.

Twelve

-▽-

ZOE

"Something feels off," Jax said after the coalition members' faces faded from the crystal globe. "You risked your ass for two weeks looking for those kids and now that you found 'em they're putting off the rescue?" He shook his head. "Doesn't add up."

"I don't know what adds up anymore," I said. We'd been writing down the ways things were different here, trying to figure out how our worlds were connected, but we hadn't gotten very far. "Maybe we should read our notes again."

He shrugged and reached for the "What We Know About Imagine" notebook next to the crystal globe.

This dimension was made with a mix of magic and science by a powerful wizard who loved Disneyland.

A magician called the game master is causing trouble by mixing magic with virtual reality. He's in this dimension but the coalition doesn't know where.

Magic is spreading out of the Magic Isle and has to be contained before we can take a shuttle back to Earth.

Real kids are being kidnapped and turned into avatars for the game.

There are more animatrons here than people.

The people seem human, except they're every color combination. (It doesn't change how they're treated or the jobs they have!)

They all speak Spanish, French and English – and most of them speak other languages too.

They all live in New Orleans, but some people work in other sectors.

They know some things about Earth, including Michael Jordan and COVID, but they don't give a straight answer when we ask about it.

There are no schools. Kids do something called Excel. They pick what they want to learn about and get matched up with somebody who's good at it.

Master Hoofer is human, but the copies are animatrons and the number might be increasing.

The mermaids can find ways out of Riskville.

"I don't know," Jax said. "I'm not seeing any patterns. You?"

"No, but I'm starting to think you're right about the coalition hiding stuff from us." I stood up and stretched my legs. They'd never been this tired or this sore. I was working the morning shift and the night shift so that I could stay inside the manor in between and look for the kids. "Why was the coalition in such a big hurry to find them if they were just gonna let 'em sit there?"

Jax tapped his pen on the open notebook page. "And why did *you* have to be the one to find them? They said they have a whole network of helpers here."

"Seems like there's a lot of things they're not telling us, like saying DeVos took a shuttle to another dimension but not answering when you asked why shuttles could go to other dimensions but not Earth."

"And saying they can't come to Orleans, but that photo of Aly, Ms. Ella, and Arthur was taken in front of Mr. Redla's golf course." He walked across the room with his hands clasped behind his back—a sign that he was trying to figure something out. So I just wrote down my next two questions for now so I wouldn't interrupt him.

If they knew DeVos was in on the game, why didn't they tell us?

Why did Ms. Ella let me work for her in the first place?!?

I had to clench my teeth to keep myself from blurting the second one out.

Jax walked back and forth a few more times and finally stopped in front of me. "What if getting transported here wasn't a freak accident? What if there's something they need us to do?"

That didn't sound right, but I thought about it before I answered. "That could be true, but they didn't ask us to do anything that somebody here can't do."

"Not yet. Just because they didn't doesn't mean they won't." He walked into the living room and I followed him. "If Ms. Ella can make food appear out of thin air, run a multimillion-dollar company, change your hair and skin color, and make a dog the size of a Hummer, why can't she send us home?"

"They said it wouldn't be safe until the runaway magic is back on Magic Isle."

"But Mr. Redla said New Orleans has always had magic. So they can't take the magic out of here but they should be able to travel here, right?"

"Maybe. But maybe there's not enough magic here or something. We don't know what they can do." I sat on the sofa. "Can you ask the kids in your next math cla—I mean demonstration?"

"I can work it in, but after what you saw at the manor, I don't think we can wait till then. By Tuesday, those kids you saw could already be turned into avatars."

I was trying not to think about the kids. They'd been in a room that wasn't much bigger than an elevator. There was a bunk bed with a mattress but no sheets or pillows, and three kids were huddled together on the top bunk. The girl was probably a few years younger than me, and the boys looked like they were only five or six years old. They all had curly black hair and bronze skin, and I wondered if they were from the same family. The boys were crying, and the girl was trying to calm them down. "But Aly said they might be able to change the avatars back into kids."

"If you were one of those kids, would 'might' be good enough? Even 'probably' isn't good enough."

"I heard the girl say she didn't want to be a cat. Maybe she saw the kid that was in DeVos's office."

Jax's eyes looked like burning coals. "We have to get them out of there." He handed me the Imagine notebook. "Draw everything you can remember about the basement, especially all the doors you passed and where the stairs and the elevator are."

"Arthur said he could get the building's blueprints. Won't they have that stuff in them?"

He handed me his pen. "I don't think we should wait for them. If we're going to save those kids, we have to do it, like, now. Tonight or tomorrow."

"By ourselves? Talk about a suicide mission." I couldn't believe he was saying something this ridiculous.

"Would you please just draw the basement? We have to at least see if we can do it."

I started to sketch everything I could remember. "But we can't get all the kids out, even if we knew where they were. And when they find out the three kids are gone, it'll be even harder to get the other ones out."

Jax frowned and paced back and forth a few times. "The kids we get out will be proof of what's going on, and then the guards can get the other kids out."

He still wasn't thinking it through. "Let's say we *can* do it. Then what? We can't sneak the kids into this building, so where are they going to stay?"

He sat in the chair across from me. "We can rent an apartment now instead of waiting until the end of the month."

"But with three kids we'd have to rent a two-bedroom apartment, and we figured out that would cost too much, remember? We have to take turns sleeping in the bed and sleeping on an air mattress in the living room."

He leaned over to look at my drawing. "We can afford a two-bedroom in Turtle Town."

"Turtle Town!" The one place I *really* didn't want to live. "Maybe we should give the coalition a couple more days."

"Maybe, but we need to be ready to roll if they don't come through." He picked up the notebook with the dollar signs on the front and opened it to the page with our revised budget. "Let's look at this again and see if we can cut anything else to give us more rent money."

Revised Monthly Budget
(based on 20 workdays a month)

Gross Income:	$3,120	
Zoe $1,920 ($480 per week)		
Jax $1,200 ($300 per week)		
New Orleans Income Tax	10.7%	$334
Savings		
3-month income cushion	(10%)	$312
Money to take home ($156 each)	(10%)	$312

Bank Fees	$10	
Liabilities		
Loan Payment to Ms. Ella	$400	
Credit Card Payment	$15	
Charitable Contributions		
Climate Change Collective	$10	
Expenses		
Rent	(30%)	$936
Utilities (included)	$0	
Groceries	$400	
Laundry	$0	
Clothing ($40 each)	$80	
Personal Care Products ($20 each)	$40	
Entertainment (5%) ($78 each)	$156	
Eating Out		
Delivery/Takeout		
Concerts/Dance Clubs		
Total Monthly Expenses:	$3,005	
Net Income: ($57.50 each)	$115	

"We can cut eating out, but we have to add money for groceries to feed the kids."

The night we ate at Coop's Place was the only time I'd felt happy since we got here. Giving up going out to dinner was going to suck, but I nodded. I mean, it *was* the right thing to do.

"And you can't go back to the manor after we get the kids out," he said, "so I need to make enough to cover everything, plus the other stuff we're gonna need."

"I can get another job. There have to be kids who want a dance or gymnastics demonstrator. Plus, I won competitions, so maybe I can be a practitioner and charge more."

"Maybe. But you have to lay low, at least until they catch Hoofer and DeVos. If they suspect you—which they will—every clown in this town will be on a Zoe hunt."

"Slash and Burns can protect me."

He set down the pen and stared at me. "Zoe, if we do this, we have to ditch them. They work for Ms. Ella. They'd never let us do this, and they definitely won't *help* us do it. Arthur said there should be at least eight people on the rescue squad."

He was right, but all I could think about was getting caught and being turned into an avatar and never seeing my family or friends again. I wanted to cry, but I knew it wouldn't help.

"Do you want to make dinner or get on the globe and look for an apartment?" he said.

I couldn't think of anything more depressing than looking for a place to live in Turtle Town at the moment, so I picked making dinner, even though it was stir-fry veggies and it would take forever to slice everything up. At least the one-pot made the rice easy. "I'll do dinner."

"Make sure you do *mise en place* before you heat up the wok."

"Meez and what?"

"Really? You're a foodie, and you don't know what *mise en place* means?"

"You could just tell me instead of insulting me, you know."

"It's French for 'everything in its place.' It means you're supposed to get all the ingredients ready before you start cooking."

"Oh." It would have been polite to thank him, but between worrying about the kids, being scared that we'd have to rescue them ourselves, and imagining living in Turtle Town, I didn't have it in me. So I dragged myself to the kitchen, turned on the local music station, and took my frustration out on the carrots and celery.

Dinner turned out pretty good, and it looked pretty with all the different-colored veggies. While we ate, we talked about how we could make more money. Jax said he could probably have as many as ten kids in a math demo, and if he did that five days a week, he could make six thousand dollars a month. That would be enough to take care of the kids and have some left to take back to LA, but where was he going to get all those new kids?

After dinner, Jax called up the apartments he'd bookmarked on the globe, but they weren't just bad—they were horrible. "Let me look at our budget again," he said. "There has to be something else we can cut."

When I opened it, I noticed there was a credit card payment for fifteen dollars a month. "What's this?" I tapped the line with my fingernail.

"That's the minimum we have to pay on the credit card every month."

"But we haven't used it."

"I used it—I had to. I was going to tell you about it. I'll pay it all myself."

"What are you talking about? Used it for what?"

"The day I had my interview with Mr. Redla, he wanted me to caddy for him, so I had to buy some clothes."

"How much did you spend?"

"A hundred seventy-five and change."

"For golf clothes?"

"And shoes. And I got the job, so it was worth it."

"Fine, but if you only pay the minimum, you'll be paying a bunch of interest. Might as well just throw that money out the window. And just so you know, you're not supposed to use more than 30 percent of the credit limit or it can trash your credit score. So do the math."

He frowned. "I'd have had to spend nine hundred dollars to be at 30 percent of our limit. But I guess I still shouldn't have spent so much."

"You shouldn't have spent anything!"

"When did you become a credit card expert?"

"When I saw my mom crying about the credit card bills my dad left her with when he took off."

He opened his calculator. "So, if I only pay the 4 percent minimum every month, it'll take twelve months to pay off and I'll pay twenty dollars in interest? Man, that shit should be illegal."

"And that's not the only thing. If you miss a payment or you're late, they jack up the interest rate."

"Damn, I didn't know."

"Well, you know now. And *now* it's time for me to show Mr. Math how credit scores work." I waved my pencil in his face just to rub it in a little. "Banks use five things to come up with your credit score. And if you don't have a good score, you can't get a loan, at least not from anybody but a loan shark."

I spelled it out for him in the notebook:

Credit Score

5 categories:

Payment history	35%
Total amount owed	30%
Length of credit history	15%
New credit	10%
Kind of credit in use	10%

He just looked at me like I had two heads.

"What?"

"I can't believe you know all this. When Ms. Ella told us we were approved for the card, you weren't even paying attention."

"Because I knew I wasn't going to use it and I didn't think you would either. Especially without telling me."

"I'm sorry, Zoe. I mean it." Then he turned back to the budget page and saw the questions I wrote about the coalition:

If they knew DeVos was in on the game, why didn't they tell us?

Why did Ms. Ella let me work for her in the first place?!?

He shook his head. "Two more reasons we shouldn't trust them."

Thirteen

-△-

JAX

The building manager at Turtle Town Terraces put an "approved" sticker on my application and slid the lease across the counter for me to sign. I'd read it on the globe when I added it to our list, so I didn't take the time to read it again before I signed it. I put $750 in cash on the counter and asked for a receipt.

She counted it and said, "The total is $2,450. First month, last month, and $200 security deposit."

"But what if our first month *is* our last month?"

"It's a three-month lease. You'll have to pay for the second month, and we'll return the last month's rent and the security deposit if the apartment passes inspection."

I'd looked at six apartments and this was the only one-bedroom we could afford. We were rescuing the kids tonight and had to have a place for them, so I pulled out the credit card and handed it to her. At least this time I knew the deal.

She scanned the card and handed it back to me with a small card that had two smiley face stickers on it. "Here are your keys. Be sure to put them somewhere convenient."

I thought she was joking, but she wasn't smiling and I wondered if she even could. "Um. Can you explain how these work?"

"New here, huh?" She pulled another card from her desk drawer. "These are the instructions."

I took a minute to read them in case I had questions. "So, we stick these on our arms and hold them in front of the keypad to unlock the door? What if it gets wet or falls off."

She frowned. "It won't fall off. Details are on our globesite." And then she walked away and went into another room.

Guess the conversation's over.

When I got back to Ms. Ella's apartment, Zoe was stuffing clothes into her roller bag. "Make sure you take everything you're gonna need," she said without looking up at me.

"Did you figure out how we're getting past your guards?"

"I think so. The north elevator at the other end of the hall goes to an underground parking garage." She sat on the suitcase to get it to close.

"Okay, but how are we going to get to that elevator without them knowing? One of them is always outside our door."

She bounced on her suitcase again.

"You know, if you roll your clothes instead of stuffing them in like garbage, you can fit in a lot more."

"So you're Martha Stewart now?" She gave me a look but dumped her stuff out onto the floor and started rolling up a T-shirt. "I'll go down the elevator with Burns, and when we get to the lobby, I'll say I forgot something. I can say I'll be right back and jump in the elevator right before it closes. And then I'll get off on the first floor and take the north elevator to the parking garage, where you'll be waiting with our roller bags."

"What if she gets on the elevator with you? Or takes the other elevator up to our floor?"

"I'll make sure she doesn't get on with me. And if she takes the other elevator to our floor, we won't be there." She was grinning like she'd just won a gold medal or something.

I nodded. I could see holes in this plan for sure, but I couldn't think of anything better. "As soon as she figures out you're not in the building, Ms. Ella will send everyone she knows out looking for us."

She pulled a blond wig out of her backpack. "*Ta-da.* They won't be looking for a blonde. And you'll be wearing this." She handed me a purple ball cap with "Geaux Tigers!" in gold lettering.

"Seriously? You think a *ball cap* will do it?"

"There's a game tomorrow and a pep rally tonight. Everybody will be wearing them. You'll blend into the crowd."

I put the cap on backward and looked in the mirror. "I don't think so."

"It'll only take us five minutes to get from the parking garage to the manor, and with so many people in the streets partying, nobody's going to notice us."

"Then why do you need blond hair?"

She rolled her eyes. "So the people at the manor don't recognize me but facial rec will still open the door." She took black pants, a white shirt, and a black bow tie out of the closet and threw them to me. "The servers at the parties wear these. If somebody sees us in the manor, we can pretend we're working at the party and got lost or something."

The reality of what we were about to do suddenly sank in, and I started getting a little keyed up. "I'm gonna pull up the manor's floor plan again on the globe. I want to draw the basement and the first floor to make sure we don't *really* get lost."

~

At eight thirty, Zoe came to my room to go over the plan one more time. A lot of things could go wrong. If DeVos's security guys or the clowns caught us, we might never get back home. I wondered how she could be so chill.

"You have everything you want to take?" she said, pointing to the clothes hanging in my closet.

"I took the most important stuff." I wasn't about to tell her I was saving room in my bag for the skateboard. "What time is it?"

"I'll see."

When she walked out, I slid the board in and filled the rest of the space with the clothes I needed the most. My backpack was already filled with soup cans, oatmeal, and boxes of mac and cheese.

"It's five till nine. Time for me to go to work," she said loud enough for Burns to hear outside the door. Softer, she said, "I'll see you in the garage." She held up her fist for a bump.

I wasn't feeling it, but I bumped her anyway. "See you in five."

Burns was standing outside when she left, and I watched through the peephole until I saw them get on the elevator. Then I counted to ten to make sure the door closed before I went out to the hall.

I pulled both our bags to the elevator, and it got there right away. I pressed the bottom button, which had a *P* on it, and hoped I could make it all the way down without stopping on another floor.

No dice—it stopped after we'd gone down a few floors and four guys in Tiger shirts got on.

"Gonna be a great game tomorrow," the tallest one said and slapped me on the back.

"Sure is," I said. I didn't even know who they were playing.

One of the other guys pushed the lobby button.

Shit.

That was the last floor I wanted it to stop on. But Burns should have been at the other end of the hall, so I just took some deep breaths and went over the plan again instead of freaking about all the ways it could get messed up.

The guys got off in the lobby and the doors closed before anyone else could get on.

Thank God.

A minute later I was in a parking garage packed with people, and just about everyone was wearing purple and gold threads. Some of them even had painted faces. I stood a few feet back from the elevator and focused my mind on an image of Zoe getting here, just like how Mr. Redla said he saw the golf ball go in the hole before he hit it. When somebody tapped me on the shoulder, I went into full-on ninja pose. But it was just Zoe.

"Let's go," she said, laughing at me. "You're as nervous as a long-tailed cat in a roomful of rocking chairs."

"Where'd you hear that one—from your granny?"

She gave me a nasty look. The blond wig was not her friend. "Lots of people say that here."

"Anyway, I thought you were coming down the elevator."

She took her bag and starting walking to the exit sign. "A clown got on it on the first floor, so I got out and took the stairs."

As soon as we were outside, we got pulled into a mob of people who looked like they were all heading to the pep rally. Good thing the manor was the same way. I grabbed Zoe's hand so we wouldn't get separated, but she pulled it back.

"What are you doing?"

"Just trying to make sure we stick together." *Damn.*

"Oh. Okay." Then she grabbed *my* hand and the purple and gold crew got us to the back of the manor in less than five minutes.

There were valet drivers parking cars nearby, but none of them paid any attention to us. "Where should we stash our stuff?"

We looked around, and the only good hiding place was between a dumpster and a grapevine big enough to park a car under. I hadn't seen any rats in Orleans yet, so I figured that spot would be okay. "How about here?"

"That should be okay," she said as she straightened her wig. "I've never seen anybody by the grapevines, and it'll be dark soon."

When she frowned, I knew she was thinking about what Robin and Arthur said about the rules changing after dark. I was, too, but there was nothing we could do about it. "Ready?"

"Ready as I'm gonna be."

I got down on my hands and knees and she stepped up to the facial recognition screen in the back door.

"Good evening, Zoe," the AI voice said.

The door opened, and we stepped into a dark and empty hallway.

Fourteen

-∇-

ZOE

We stood still to let our eyes adjust to the dark, but it didn't help.

Damn it!

"You said they had track lights," Jax whispered.

"They do. They're not on," I whispered back. The track lighting was always turned on when the overhead lights were on, and I'd just figured they were on all the time. This time I reached for Jax's hand. "The door's at the end of the hall."

He gave my hand a quick squeeze. "Put your other hand out in front."

I did, and as we slowly started down the hall, I prayed we wouldn't run into anything but the door at the other end. We knew where the security cameras were but didn't know if there were hidden audio sensors, so we agreed we'd only talk when we had to and then we'd whisper.

As we made our way toward the door, I could hear drums, but I couldn't tell if they were upstairs or part of the pep rally outside. When my hand finally touched the door, I ran my hand up the right side of it, feeling for the button that opened it, but nothing was there. I tried again, slower this time. Finally, my fingers landed on the bump, and when I pushed it, the door slid open.

Deep breaths.

The hall was almost as dark as the tunnel, and the torch lights on both walls were making shadows that looked too much like the ghosts I'd danced with. They say there's nothing there in the dark that isn't there in the light, but I was having a very hard time believing that right now.

Focus. We can do this.

I nodded toward the elevator on our left. If it opened for me, we'd be on our way to the basement, for better or for worse.

Jax crouched down next to me and I held up my hand to activate the facial rec. A few seconds later, the doors opened and we got on, keeping our faces turned away from the camera above the door. Jax pressed "B" and the doors closed.

As the elevator went down, we heard screaming from below.

Oh my God. "Should we take the stairs instead?"

Too late. The doors were already opening, and in the sprawling basement there was a large cage on wheels that was filled with screaming kids. A miniature horse was pulling the cage, and a clown was leading it. I gasped and Jax clamped his hand over my mouth and jerked me away from the door.

We hid in the corner of the elevator until they turned down one of the tunnels. The map we'd been able to piece together showed that the basement had tunnels that went in every direction, including up and down, and some of them looked like they went under the street to who knows where. Jax took his hand off my mouth and pointed out the door.

No turning back now.

We got out and headed for the tunnel where I'd found the kids two days ago—and where I prayed they still were. I thought I'd turned down the second tunnel on the left, but now I wasn't so sure. Nothing looked the same at night. But when we got to the turn, I took it anyway.

Please be it.

This tunnel had torches burning in wrought iron holders on the wall, and it smelled like ammonia. I scrunched up my nose to try to block the smell and forced my feet to keep moving.

Squeak.

I froze. *What was that?* I turned to Jax, who looked as freaked out as I was.

"How much farther?" he whispered.

"I'm not sure."

Then we heard it again, only louder.

"Shit," Jax said. "Rats."

Holy . . . "Are you sure?"

"Let's just get this done." He jogged ahead and I followed, looking for the door I'd seen the last time.

Then Jax stopped and pointed at the square door on his right. I stood on my tiptoes and peeked in.

"They're in there," I said. Then I looked closer. "The girl has paws."

But Jax didn't hear me. He was waving a torch back and forth across the tunnel as the squeaking got louder.

Shit, shit, shit.

I pulled the locksmith pick from my jeans pocket and wished I could do the job without putting my ear against the door, which like the walls, was covered with furry green slime. But there was no avoiding it—I had to listen for the click.

Shlurp.

It sounded like I'd just stuck my ear in a bowl of snails, but I forced myself not to think about what the disgusting goo was made of and moved the pick around until I found the sweet spot. *Thank you, Uncle Al, for teaching me this shit.* Now I just needed to open the door without making the kids scream.

I took a few deep breaths, just like I'd do in a gymnastics competition, and slowly pushed it open. The kids were whispering to each other in Spanish, and I held my finger in front of my lips, hoping they knew what it meant.

The girl saw me first. She looked scared, but she didn't scream.

"Mi nombre es Zoe," (My name is Zoe,) I whispered. "Puedo ayudarte." (I can help you.)

She wrapped her arms around the two little boys. "Debemos ser valientes, como los superhéroes," (We must be brave, like superheroes,) she said to them.

The boys nodded and climbed down from the top bunk.

"Yo sé de los payasos y del juego," (I know about the clowns and the game) I said, just loud enough for her to hear me, "Mi amigo Jax y yo te podemos ayudar." (Me and my friend Jax can help you.)

She looked like she didn't trust me, but she followed me out into the hall anyway, holding the little boys' hands.

Jax had two torches now and was sweeping them both back and forth across the tunnel.

Oh my God.

The light was reflecting what looked like hundreds of beady eyes.

The girl gasped and stood in front of the boys.

"Run!" Jax said. The rats were just a few feet in front of him.

"What about you?"

"I'll catch up with you outside." One of the pairs of eyes almost got by him. "*Run*!"

The girl picked up one of the boys and I picked up the other one and we made a run for the elevator. We didn't stop till we got to the main cavern, where I made sure nobody was out there before we ran the rest of the way. I pushed the button and turned around to keep an eye out.

Please please please get here before the rats.

When the door finally opened, we jumped on. Within a few seconds, we were on the first floor. We didn't need facial rec to get out of the manor, so we raced through the tunnel all the way to the back door. I wanted to wait for Jax, but when I opened the door the sun was setting, and like the coalition told us, the rules changed after dark. Even though the lot was still filled with cars, there was no one around.

Damn it.

I'd been counting on the streets being crowded with people from the pep rally, but there was nothing I could do about that mistake now. I got my backpack and roller bag from behind the dumpster and took a quick look at Jax's map of the route we picked to Turtle Terrace.

The girl reached for the handle of Jax's bag. "¿Me llevo ésto?" (Should I take this?)

"Por favor." I forced a smile even though I was scared. "¿Cuál es tu nombre?" (What is your name?)

"Mi nombre es Maria." She pointed to Jax's backpack. "¿Ésta también?" (This, too?)

I decided to leave it for Jax. I was hoping that taking everything except his backpack would let him know we made it out. "No. Let's go now." It was getting darker by the minute and the wig was hot and scratchy so I tossed it into the dumpster.

As we walked through the parking lot, I did my best to pretend I wasn't scared. There was literally nobody else in sight. We could have walked right down the middle of the street, but Slash and Burns were definitely looking for me by now, so we stayed close to the buildings and quietly made our way, block after block, as the darkness closed in. I kept looking over my shoulder, hoping to see Jax.

When we passed the Henny Penny B&B, I knew that Turtle Town was just a block away. I looked around, worried now that we *would* see someone since we were breaking curfew. Nobody ever told us what happened when people got caught, but I was just as scared of being caught by the guards as I was of being caught by the clowns, so I stopped at the end of every building to make sure the coast was clear.

Where are you, Jax?

We finally made it to Creek Street, and when we turned the corner, Turtle Terraces was right across the road. It was the ugliest building I'd ever seen. I looked back again to see if Jax would appear, but the street was still empty.

Maybe he went a different way and beat us back to the apartment.

After looking both ways two more times, I led the way across the street and into the front door. The lobby was empty, and there was nobody at the front desk. There also wasn't an elevator.

Great. The key sticker Jax told me to put on my wrist said "20-R"—we'd have to walk up twenty flights of stairs. I hoped the boys could do it.

As we made our way up, I could hear music coming from some of the floors and smell all kinds of food, but we didn't see anybody. Maybe everybody stayed in their apartments after dark, which made me want to sprint up the stairs. But we still had eight floors to go, and the boys were already slowing down. *Patience, Zoe.*

When we finally made it to the twentieth floor the door marked 20-R was right next to the stairwell.

I smiled at Maria. "We made it."

I opened the door, hoping Jax would be on the other side, but when I turned on the light, nobody was home. Just the roaches that disappeared in between the floorboards. I wanted to cry.

I can't do this myself.

I forced my face to smile. I didn't want to scare Maria and the twins. "¿Tienen hambre?" (Are you hungry?)

The boys nodded like bobbleheads. "Sí, Zoe," Maria said.

I took the family-size can of vegetable soup out of my backpack, along with the compostable bowls and the five spoons I borrowed from Ms. Ella's. "You can wash your hands while I heat this up."

Maria led the boys into the tiny bathroom, and I washed a saucepan I found in the cupboard and poured the soup into it. The only food in the apartment was what I had in my backpack, so what were the roaches after? Then I saw it—under the green chair was a partially eaten rat that was bigger than a Pomeranian.

Oh my God. I had to jerk my head away so I wouldn't puke.

I rummaged around under the sink until I found a trash bag and a dustpan and held my breath as I scooped up what was left of the giant rodent. After I tied a knot in the bag and dropped it in the trash chute outside the door, a terrible question popped into my head.

If the rats in the tunnel were as big as this one, what chance did Jax have?

Fifteen

-△-

JAX

My biceps were cramping and sweat was running down my arms, making it tough to hold onto the torches. But I kept waving them back and forth, hoping Zoe and the kids would get on the elevator before my arms gave out.

Hold the line, dude. Just hold the line.

Then I saw the rat.

Seriously?

It went for my arm, and when I jumped back I dropped one of the torches.

"Damn it!"

I reached for it, but his buddies all of a sudden showed up—hundreds of them—and I was pretty much surrounded within seconds. Holding on to the torch I still had, I jumped through the door to the kids' cell and up onto the top bunk. When I waved the torch out over the room, it was filled with the biggest rats I'd ever seen.

Holy shit.

Some of them were trying to climb up the bed frame, but they kept slipping back down. And some of them were trying to climb the walls. Most of them couldn't do it, but a few smaller ones made it halfway up, and I was ready to charbroil them if they tried to jump on the bed.

Shreeeeee.

The sound of a whistle almost broke my eardrum, but the rats actually started running toward it.

Uh-oh.

I couldn't go back the way I came if somebody was out there, but where would I end up if I went the way the rats came from? I didn't know, but if whoever blew the whistle had a key, I could get locked in. I needed to come up with some kind of diversion and get the hell out.

Think.

I looked around and then noticed the dirty blanket I was sitting on.

That'll work.

I used the torch to set it on fire and then propped the torch up on the mattress. Then I booked it down the tunnel as fast as my Nike Airs would go. Every time I got to a torch, I ducked down to go under it so no one would see me blocking the light. After about thirty yards, I heard someone yell, "Fire!"

I kept moving, but the stone floor was getting wetter with every step.

Where is this taking me?

I hoped it wasn't to the river.

Behind me, the tunnel was filled with smoke, so I grabbed another torch off the wall—I figured no one would be able to see it through the smoke. I followed the tunnel down a slope to a stream, where I seemed to run out of options. No way was I getting in the water, knowing those rats must have crawled out of there. I moved the torch around, looking for some kind of a secret doorway.

Nothing.

I could hear guys shouting on the other side of the smoke wall, and if I didn't find a way out, they'd have me in minutes. I looked at the stream again.

No freakin' way.

There had to be some other way. I pushed and poked the wall and felt a hole about the size of a baseball. When I held the torch closer, I could see a bunch of holes in the wall that went up as far as I could see. I didn't want to leave the torch behind, but I didn't have any choice. I'd need both hands to climb. I also didn't want to leave evidence behind either, so I dug the fingers of my right hand into the highest hole I could reach, pitched the torch into the stream and started up the wall.

Climbing gyms aren't my thing, so I moved pretty slowly, but it didn't take long till I saw a yellow light above me. I was about twenty feet up, and after a few more feet, I felt a grate above my head. I stayed still for a few minutes, listening, and when I didn't hear any more voices, I shoved the grate up and climbed out.

I was in a parking lot full of cars, but nobody was around. After putting the grate back in as quietly as I could, I crept between the cars, trying to figure out where the hell I was. When I got to the edge of the lot, I could hardly believe it—the dumpster where we hid our stuff was a few yards in front of me. I was right behind the manor. My backpack was where I left it, but the roller bags and Zoe's pack were gone, and I just hoped that meant they were on their way to the apartment. I pulled the Turtle Terraces map out of my pocket, and just then a high-pitched siren went off. In seconds, the parking lot started filling up with clowns.

Damn it.

I dived into the grapevine and looked out through the leaves. Clowns were pouring out the back door of the manor. There were hundreds of them, just like the rats. Maybe even a thousand. Then a spotlight lit up a balcony and Master Hoofer stepped into the light. The siren stopped.

"Find them!" he shouted, and the clowns took off running in every direction.

Chills ran up my arms. I had to get to the apartment. But with all the clowns around, I couldn't go down to the street.

Think, dude.

Two of Imagine's moons were rising and that made it easier to see, but that meant it made it easier to see *me*, too. I looked around and noticed that DeVos's privacy wall was almost as high as the roof next door. I remembered the view I had of New Orleans from Ms. Ella's castle—the rooftops were pretty close together in this part of town and got tighter the closer you got to Turtle Town. Maybe I could make it to the apartment without touching the ground.

I crawled along the top of the wall, and when I got to the end, it was about a three-foot jump up to the roof. The clowns in the parking lot had all scattered, so I backed up a few yards and took a running jump onto it. This house had a privacy wall, too, and since nobody was around, I dropped from the roof, ran across the top of the wall and jumped onto the next roof. I did the same thing for the next few blocks, and the roofs kept getting higher. By the time

I got to Big Easy Street, I was on top of a building that was at least twelve floors. As I stared at the street below, trying to figure out what to do next, a bunch of clowns ran out of a high-rise across the street. One of them had a blond wig in his hand.

Zoe's?

I ducked down in case they looked up. I had to cross Big Easy to get to Turtle Town, but there was no way across from here.

"Close this road," one of the clowns said. "Nobody goes in or out of Turtle Town until we find them."

I scrambled around on my hands and knees looking for a door. Roofs have doors so people can do maintenance, so there had to be one.

Come on, where is it? Where is it?

Then my hand found a handle. When I leaned away a little, I could see the outline of a door made of the same metal as the rest of the roof. I yanked on the handle, but it didn't budge. I needed a Plan B.

I crawled to the edge of the roof to see what was happening. Clowns were pulling up on scooters, ponies, golf carts and adult-size tricycles and making a barricade down the middle of the street. I remembered Mr. Redla's advice to take in all the information as if I'd never heard it or seen it before. It sounded impossible when he first said it, but he said that's how he figured out the obstacles on the side nine and in the courtroom. So I tried to take everything in around me.

Big Easy was lined with clowns in both directions, as far as I could see. I counted the rows of windows in the building across the street and calculated that the building I was on was about ten stories. Maybe there was a rope or something I could tie together to rappel down. There was a pile of broken boards and a few short pieces of rope on the other side of the roof, but nothing I could use to get down.

I looked down over this side of the building and saw a dark alley. It smelled like dead fish. *Nasty.*

Then I noticed the scaffolding. There were four planks, each about six feet long, and they were hanging from ropes hooked to the rooftop. The highest one was about fifteen feet down. It looked like there were a couple floors between the planks.

Creeeak.

I jerked around and saw the rooftop door opening, and two clowns carrying long silver swords climbed out.

Shit!

I dropped down to the top plank, praying I could eventually climb back up, but when I looked up, one of them was standing right over me.

"Get him!"

My mind raced as I looked at the planks below. They looked sort of like stairs.

Yeah, stairs for somebody about fifty feet tall.

And then I remembered my board.

Perfect!

I yanked it out of my bag and ran as fast as I could toward the end of the plank. About two feet from the end, I dropped my board, and angling my body to land on the plank below, I ollied off the edge.

Boom.

Pain ripped through my legs, but I managed to hold on and ollie off the other end of the wood. *Big air—stay loose, dude.* And I did.

Bam.

Ducking between the scaffolding ropes, I sped forward and ollied into the air again, just barely catching the edge of the third plank. One more to go.

This one was farther away, and I crouched down to get ready to ollie and jumped as high as I could. It was the most air I'd ever caught.

Tight core, soft knees, breathe.

My front wheels kissed the end of the plank and the board spun out from under me.

Oh no.

My pack pulled me backward and I was falling fast.

Spin, dude!

I threw my head back, pulled my knees in tight and forced my body to rotate.

Splat.

I landed on my back, but it felt like I smacked water instead of pavement. And then the rotten fish smell hit me like a ton of bricks and I started gagging. I was lying in a dumpster filled with fish heads.

I climbed out like the dumpster was filled with sharks—live ones—and tried to scrape off the pieces stuck to my clothes. Then I spotted my board a few yards away. The clowns would be here in no time, so I ignored the rest of the fish stuck to me and the pain making my legs scream, threw down my board and flew down the alley.

I was heading north instead of south to Turtle Town—I had to find a way to the apartment that wasn't blocked off—but how was I going to do that without anybody seeing me? I looked over my shoulder and nobody was following me, so I turned left toward

Riskville. Maybe I could get to Turtle Town from High Street. That entrance might be blocked too, but I had to try.

Both moons were overhead now and bright enough that it looked almost like daytime. I ducked into the shadow of a tall building to think about my plan again. There was no curfew outside of New Orleans, but Riskville was at least eight blocks away. Could I make it that far without being seen? And how was curfew enforced anyway? Did the guards patrol the streets? Were there hidden cameras? Did they *already* see me? And what about the clowns that saw me skate down the scaffolding? Were they looking for me?

A ton of questions and no answers. Mr. Redla said that when you're trying to solve a problem, you should start with what you know, so I made myself stop thinking about questions and think about what I knew.

Okay. I'm at the corner of Sweet and Tart streets. The apartment is five blocks south of here. Big Easy Street is blocked. The High Street entrance to Turtle Town is about a mile from here and might be blocked. If the New Orleans guards catch me outside, they'll arrest me. If the clowns catch me—wait, skip that part. Should I just turn myself in to the guards before the clowns catch me?

Armed guys in uniforms didn't seem to like me too much, but it wasn't like I could expect to find a friend right now.

Wait—maybe I can.

The Redlas lived a couple blocks from here—Mr. Redla would know what to do.

I picked up my board and ran across Sweet Street, and two minutes later I was standing on their front porch. I rang the bell and one of the androids that worked for them opened the door.

"Hello, Jax. It is after curfew."

"I know. Can I come in? I need to talk to Mr. Redla."

It shook its silver head. “Mr. Redla is not here.”

“How about Mrs. Redla or, um, Cheyenne?”

“No one is home.”

“Can I wait for them inside? The way I do when I’m here to work with Cheyenne and get here before her?” I’d figured out that I could talk androids into things sometimes if I used logic, giving them an example of something they’d seen. And this time it worked.

I walked in and went to the kitchen to wait. I would have sat in the entry hall outside the living room, but the slime and the fish stink from the tunnel were stuck to me. That situation wasn’t going to get any better till I could get a shower.

The android came back with a portable globe and handed it to me. “You are wanted.”

I thought he was talking about my demonstrations—I had a waiting list about three blocks long. But then I looked at the screen and saw a video of me crossing the parking lot behind DeVos’s manor. And then I read the banner underneath it: “Wanted: Suspected Arsonist.”

Holy shit.

Sixteen

-▽-

ZOE

The kids fell asleep right after the soup, but with the roaches and the rats and worrying about Jax, there was no way *I* was going to sleep. The metal folding chair was the only piece of furniture that didn't make my skin crawl, so that's where I sat. I looked at my watch again: 5:15. It would be light out soon. Not that it mattered, since there were no windows in here and we couldn't go outside. The dim light over the kitchen sink made the whole room look like a black-and-white photo, and not in a cool way. I stared at the mostly empty refrigerator. *What am I going to give the kids for breakfast?* Jax had most of the food in his pack. *Where are you, Jax?*

Bam bam bam.

I froze.

Jax?

No, he had a key. And even if he didn't, he probably wouldn't pound the door like a caveman. When Maria walked into the living room rubbing her eyes, I put my finger to my lips, and she nodded and stood in front of the bedroom door with her arms crossed. My heart was racing.

Please don't be a clown.

More pounding. "Open up. It's Slash."

It sounded like him, but without a peephole, how could I know for sure? I walked over to the door. "Prove it."

"What? This isn't a game, miss. You're in a heap of trouble." Definitely sounded like Slash.

"With who?"

"Open the door and I'll tell you."

"Ms. Ella lied to us. Why should I trust you?"

"Because you can't stay in there forever, and the city is crawling with clowns and guards and they're all looking for you and Jax. You for trespassing and Jax for arson."

I yanked open the door. "Arson? What are you talking about?"

He came in and closed the door. "I'll tell you on the way to the castle. Get your stuff. Burns is waiting for us out back."

"What about the kids?" I pointed to Maria, who was still guarding the bedroom door.

"What the . . . " He shook his head. "You pulled it off?"

The twins stumbled out of the bedroom and stood behind their sister.

"How many are there?"

"Dozens, maybe more."

"Here?" He looked around the room as if they might all pop out of the floorboards where the roaches went.

"No. At the manor. There are only three here."

"Well, I'll be damned." He grinned and then wiped it off with his fist. "Plenty of room in the carriage for all of us."

I picked up my backpack. "What happened to Jax?"

"He can tell you himself. He's at Ms. Ella's. Let's get a move on."

We followed him down the stairs as I reassured Maria in Spanish that we were going to a safe place, without completely believing it myself. But between the clowns, the guards, and the coalition, it wasn't much of a contest. Even if Ms. Ella *had* been lying to us. Maybe she had a good reason.

When Slash and Burns escorted us to the front door of the castle, the twins were still yawning, but Maria was wide awake and smiling. "Disneyland?"

"Looks like it, huh?" I said. I explained what I knew about Imagine and the wizard who made it and realized I still didn't know if Maria was from Earth or somewhere else.

"We'll be waiting right here for you," Burns said as she opened the door.

Maria's mouth fell open when she saw the giant trees in the hallway. "Amazing," she said in English.

"You speak English?"

She nodded. "A little."

What else don't I know?

When we got to the lab, Ms. Ella and Jax were waiting for us outside, along with a tall man that looked like the photo I saw of Mr. Redla.

Ms. Ella smothered me with a hug. "We were worried sick about you." She stood back and looked me up and down. "Thank goodness you weren't hurt. What you did was very brave and very foolish."

Can't argue with that.

"This is Mr. Redla," Jax said.

He smiled. "I'm relieved you're all safe."

That reminded me that I didn't introduce the kids yet. "This is Maria and her brothers, Manny and Marco."

Ms. Ella knelt down to be eye-level with the boys. "How about some breakfast?"

"Sí, sí," (Yes, yes,) the boys said, and Ms. Ella took them by the hands and led the way into the lab.

Whew. Seeing the table instead of the swings made me feel better. And still better, the table was covered with pastries and all kinds of fruit. I almost forgot why we were here.

"How'd you find us?" I asked Ms. Ella, but Jax answered.

"I told 'em where you were. The clowns were chasing me and I went to Mr. Redla's for help. That's when I found out it was a race between the clowns and the guards to find us."

"Why the guards? For breaking curfew? Or did you really start a fire?"

"I set the blanket on fire to make a smoke shield. There was nothing else but the mattress down there that could burn." He shook his head. "Wanted for arson—that's messed up." He picked up a doughnut hole and dipped it in caramel sauce.

"To hear Ms. DeVos tell it," Mr. Redla said, "the arsonist put the lives of the city's most respected dignitaries at risk by setting the manor on fire during one of the biggest fundraising events of the year."

Jax rolled his eyes. "Bullsh—" He looked at the twins. "Bologna."

The twins both laughed. Obviously, they knew some English, too. At least the swear words.

"Don't be shy," Ms. Ella said, taking a slice of watermelon from one of the trays. "Dig in."

"Solo tomen uno," (Only take one,) Maria said to the boys. They nodded but didn't look happy about it. "Si lo terminan, pueden tener otro." (If you finish it, you can have another.)

Ms. Ella's southern charm and Mr. Redla's questions brought out more about the kids in five minutes than I'd learned all night. Maria was nine, her brothers were five, and they lived in Mexico. Maria said her bike got a flat tire when she was riding home from school and a man and woman in a Land Rover gave her a ride home. But when they got there, instead of dropping her off, the man went inside and took her brothers. He gave them candy and they fell asleep, and when they woke up, they were in a cave with dozens of other kids. Some of them were kids who disappeared from their village.

Ms. Ella patted Maria's hand. "Don't you worry. We'll rescue them when we stop the game."

"You found a way to stop the game?" I said with a mouth full of chocolate croissant.

"We think so. But to do it, we have to find the control center, which I'm sure the game master and his minions are guarding."

"Where have you looked?" Mr. Redla said.

"We've scoured Magic Isle and he's not here," Ms. Ella said. "He has too much magic to survive in New Orleans, so he has to be in one of the other sectors."

"Do *you* have more magic now than you used to have?" Jax said.

"Yes, but not in the sense that you might think. It's complicated."

"What I want to know is why you used to be able to go to New Orleans but now you say you can't."

Mr. Redla chuckled. "Maybe you should think about a career in law."

Ms. Ella sighed. "The short answer is that ever since the game master started the game, our magic is unpredictable in the sectors that aren't totally governed by the laws of magic."

"I'm listening," Jax said, "but I'm not following."

"Let me put it like this. If we go there, maybe everything will be fine. But if our magic takes an unexpected turn, we could hurt people." She smiled. "The good news is that we've been able to pull the magic tendrils from all the sectors but Riskville. And that means, as soon as we stop the game, it will be safe to send you home."

I could hardly believe what I was hearing. Last night I thought I'd be bitten by rats or kidnapped by clowns, and this morning I find out we might be going home any day? I felt a little lightheaded.

"The bad news," Mr. Redla said, "is there are warrants out for your arrest. None of the guard reports mention three missing kids, of course." He frowned. "Devos and Hoofer are making sure all the attention is on you two."

It seemed like Mr. Redla and Ms. Ella seriously cared. "Can you help us?"

"I can change your appearances," Ms. Ella said, "but you won't be able to go back to your jobs. I'll make you new IDs with new names so you can apply for new jobs."

"But we won't be here long enough to need new jobs, will we?"

"Maybe not, but we can't be sure, so you should start looking for new jobs right away."

"My firm can defend you," Mr. Redla said, "but Jax needs to stop doing his math demonstrations for now, except with Cheyenne."

Great. I knew I couldn't go back to my job, but now both of us were out of work?

"Don't worry, kids," Ms. Ella said and stood up. "Now, Jax, what color do you want to be?"

He looked a little embarrassed. “Uh, how about purple, I guess, with green eyes and,” he shrugged, “let’s go with blue hair.”

Ms. Ella waved her hand in front of him, and he changed just like that.

The kids gasped.

“Nothing to be afraid of, kids,” Mr. Redla said. “Just some good old-fashioned magic.”

Ms. Ella turned to me. “What about you, Zoe?”

I picked bronze skin, green eyes, and red hair, and the kids gasped again.

Maria asked for bright yellow skin, orange hair, and brown eyes, which Ms. Ella gave her, but she still had paws.

“We need to do a little more magic to get your hands back,” she said, “so keep them tucked in your pocket for now.”

“Thank you,” Maria said and turned to her brothers. “¿Cómo quieren aparecer mientras estamos aquí?” (What do you want to look like while we’re here?)

They said they wanted to look like Jax, so they both got green eyes, blue hair, and purple skin. Now they looked like they were *his* brothers.

Ms. Ella said Slash and Burns would take us to her apartment because, even with our new appearances, we wouldn’t be safe until DeVos and Hoofer were in custody.

I almost started to cry. Thank God we weren’t going back to the roach motel.

Mr. Redla stood up. “Don’t talk to anyone on your way to the apartment, and don’t use your real names. You look different but you sound the same, and the clowns are foolish, but not stupid.” He patted Jax on the shoulder. “I’ll pick you up tomorrow morning for Cheyenne’s demonstration. At least you’ll still have one student.”

Ms. Ella steered us toward the door and pressed an envelope into my hand. "Some money to buy the kids clothes, but not until we say it's safe to go out."

Outside, Slash and Burns were standing next to the robo-carriage and we all climbed in. The streets were empty—it was only seven o'clock—and the kids stared out the windows at the tall buildings while Jax told us about his skateboard escape.

"Best tricks of my life and biggest air, too, and nobody there to see it."

He looked pretty bummed, but I couldn't help roasting him a little. "What do you call the one where you land in the fish heads?"

He laughed. "Fine, but right up until then, it was dope."

"Uh-huh." Actually, I believed him, but I wasn't about to tell *him* that.

When the robo-carriage pulled up in front of the high-rise, Burns opened the door. "Remember, don't talk until you're inside the apartment."

Maria repeated the warning to her brothers in Spanish, and we all got out.

As we walked into the beautiful lobby filled with vases of fresh flowers, I felt like I was dreaming. And with any luck, in a few minutes I would be.

Seventeen

JAX

After a day and a night inside, Maria was still wandering around the apartment and looking out windows like she was seeing for the first time. "So many trees," she said. The twins stopped wrestling to look, too, but then Manny poked Marco in the stomach and they started again.

"Are there forests where you live?" she asked.

"Yeah, but not like that," I said.

The boys rolled across the rug and into the couch, where Zoe was sitting cross-legged and frowning at her notebook.

"¡Basta!" (Enough!) Maria said. "No más lucha libre hoy." (No more wrestling today.)

I remembered being stuck inside at their age when smoke from wildfires poured into the city. "Too bad we can't go to a park."

"¡Quiero ir al parque!" (I want to go to the park!) Manny shouted.

"¡Yo también!" (Me too!) Marco yelled.

Oops.

"¡Niños! Iremos al parque cuando la Sra. Ella diga que es seguro." (Boys! We'll go to the park when Ms. Ella says it's safe.)

The boys both started crying.

Crap. "How about if we play a very cool game called kick golf?"

Maria translated and the crying stopped even though they had no idea what kick golf was. I didn't either—I just made it up—but I looked around and found some papers in the recycling bin. After crushing them into balls, I set one on the floor and kicked it with the side of my foot. "You can only touch the ball with your foot."

"Solo puedes tocar la pelota con el pie," Maria translated.

I moved a couple dining room chairs to the middle of the living room and pulled two more out from under the table. "You have to kick your ball through all the chair legs." Then I turned the empty waste basket next to the front door onto its side. "And to win, you have to kick your ball into this basket."

As soon as Maria translated the rules, Manny and Marco started kicking the paper balls and screaming and laughing so much I thought they were going to pee their pants. Zoe looked annoyed. "We makin' too much noise?"

"What?" She looked up from her notebook.

"Are we being too loud?"

She shook her head. "I'm just trying to figure out how we're going to make a menu on our budget. Everything's so expensive."

"You want me to take a shot at it while you play with the kids?"

Maria rushed into the living room. "I'm so sorry. You don't have to play with them. I can watch them."

"¡No!" They wrapped around my legs and almost knocked me over.

"I have to figure out how to do this," Zoe said. "But maybe you and Maria can find some clothes for the kids on the globe."

"Okay, but tell me if you want help. For real."

She tapped her notebook with her pen. "I'll take any tips if you have 'em."

"Um, sure." This was the first time she ever asked for my advice. "Okay, I got a few things you can do to make the money go further."

She turned the page in her notebook. "Ready."

"Buy fruit and vegetables when they're in season and look at what the store has on sale before you figure out what to make that week."

She wrote it down. "What else?"

"Pick recipes that are mostly vegetarian, with meat or chicken mixed in. Like a big salad with chicken strips instead of a chicken breast with a salad on the side." I walked back and forth trying to think of what else I could tell her. "Beans and rice and pasta are cheap and filling, and we can make a bunch of different dinners with them." The kids were still trying to push me over.

"That's good for now," she said. "Thanks."

I peeled the boys off of me. "Wanna see how the globe works?"

"Sí, sí," (Yes, yes,) they both said.

We went into Ms. Ella's office and I asked the globe to show us a map of New Orleans. They were all blown away by the city, but they really wanted to see the rides in the park sectors. "All right, all right. We have all day to shop. Might as well have some fun first."

There were security cameras all over Imagine, which Mr. Redla said was one of the reasons the crime rate was so low, but I thought it was kind of sketchy. He said as far as Imagine's directors were concerned, it wasn't an invasion of privacy as long as the cameras recorded just video or just audio. It didn't make any sense to me, but I was getting used to that here.

"Does Imagine have Adventureland?" Maria said.

"Sort of. It's called Riskville and the rides aren't exactly the same."

She passed on what I said to Manny and Marco. "My brothers want to know if there's a tree house."

I clicked on the camera icon closest to the rundown tree house Zoe and I had run by. "There is, but it's not like the one in Disneyland." I turned on the panorama effect so it looked like we were walking around the tree. The guys clapped and jumped up and down.

From this camera angle, we could see the mermaids sitting on rocks.

"Are they animatrons?" Maria said.

"Believe it or not, they're real."

"¡De ninguna manera!" (No way!)

She leaned in to get a closer look, and I switched to full globe to make the picture bigger. It looked like the mermaids were hassling the people on the boat going by.

"I wish I could hear them," Maria said.

"Las sirenas no pueden hablar," Manny said.

Maria laughed. "Manny believes mermaids are real, but he does not believe they talk."

That gave me an idea. "Maybe I can get the audio from the boat dock." I'd hacked into the audio system at the manor, so I figured it wouldn't be that hard to get into the audio feed for Riskville. The kids jumped up and down while I gave commands to the globe and finally got into the main menu. When I picked the speaker icon on the dock, we could see the mermaids and hear the boat captain.

"Sick! It worked!"

I wondered how many people did this same thing to seriously spy on each other.

"What's your name, sailor?" the mermaid with red hair called out to the boat.

The captain laughed. "Won't catch *this* sea dog with that old trick." He turned to the people onboard. "You see, friends, if a mermaid knows your name, she can use it like a charm and no mortal can resist her."

Guys on the boat started shouting their names or maybe their friends' names, but the boat took off before any of them could jump overboard. Then the mermaids started to sing and dance, and Manny and Marco were glued to the globe. What caught *my* eye, though, were the clowns going in a back door of the tree house. I looked for the audio icon for the tree house, but there wasn't one.

Hmmm. Haven't run into this *one before.*

"Hold on, guys. We'll come back to the mermaids in a minute." I picked up the microphone outside the Temple of Gloom and turned the volume all the way up. "I'm trying to hear the clowns." I couldn't hear anything at first, but then three clowns walked out the back door.

"The master wants new avatars by next week," the tallest one said. "He doesn't care if we lose some in training."

The boys didn't understand the English, but Maria did. "¡Ay, Dios mío!" (Oh, my God!) she said and started crying. "They have my friend."

I held out a tissue for her, but she just wiped her eyes with the backs of her paws.

We watched for a few more minutes, and when no more clowns showed up, I went out to the living room to tell Zoe.

"We need to tell Ms. Ella," she said. "And not on the globe, since it's not a secure channel."

"But she said not to leave the apartment," Maria said.

"We don't have to. Slash or Burns will tell her."

Maria grabbed Zoe's hands with her paws. "Please ask her to save my friend."

"I will."

I just hoped we weren't too late.

Eighteen

-∇-

ZOE

Being stuck inside for a week sucks even if the place you're stuck in is a fancy apartment. All I wanted to do was go outside. The sky was bright green today and the streets were filled with people celebrating Vendredi Gras, which is sort of like Fat Tuesday in Earth's New Orleans, but here it's Fat Friday. Every Friday for the whole summer, they close a bunch of streets and have a big party with bands and food trucks from all the best restaurants. I couldn't believe I had to miss the first one.

"Will you braid my hair?" Maria was standing in the bedroom door holding my comb.

Annoyed that she didn't ask me if she could use it, I put down my notebook. "Okay. How many?"

"Ten!"

"How about four?"

“Sí.”(Yes) “Four.”

She plopped down in front of me and dropped a handful of elastic hair bands on the floor. I wasn’t used to having a shadow, and it was getting on my nerves.

“Did you see all those people outside at the big party?” She turned her head around to look at me.

Of course I saw them. “Keep still or your braids will be crooked.”

“Some people are wearing costumes!”

“Yeah. I saw that.”

“Maybe we can go next Friday.”

“I *hope* so.” And then I felt guilty. *All I should be hoping for is getting home.*

“Do you want to play a game?”

The last thing I wanted to do was play a game. “Jax is using the globe to make a new résumé.”

“We could play with the cards I found.”

“I have to work on my résumé, too.”

She frowned.

“How about if we play something after dinner?”

“But we didn’t even have lunch yet.”

Patience, Zoe. As I wrapped the elastic band around the last braid, I wondered if I was this annoying when I was nine. “All done.”

She stood up but didn’t leave. “I’m bored.”

“There’s going to be a parade this afternoon. The view from the living room window will be better than if we were down on the sidewalk.”

She smiled a little. “Will you watch it, too?”

“If I get my résumé done before then.”

“Okay. Work fast.”

I nodded. Anything I said could turn into another conversation, and I really needed some me time. When she went back to the living room, I got out my old résumé and compared it with Jax's, which Ms. Ella had said was *perfect.* We both had some good job experience, but the way he wrote his sounded better, and he didn't make any mistakes. Ms. Ella circled two misspelled words on mine—I had *an* instead of *and* and *there* instead of *their.* I said the first one was a typo, but Ms. Ella said that in her book it was still a mistake. As for using the wrong spelling of *there,* she suggested that I write this sentence ten times so I wouldn't make the mistake again: "*They're* going to a party at *their* friend's house, and they have to take a train to get *there*."

After working on my résumé for more than an hour and changing the way I described my work experience a dozen times, I was happy it was ready to be typed. I went to the office to see if Jax was finished with the globe and was just about to go in when I heard him say, "The total was $2,650. They made me pay three months, plus a security deposit."

WHAT? We only had enough money for one month. I stood outside, waiting to hear what else he said.

"Cash for one month and credit for the rest."

I couldn't stand it anymore and went in. "*You used the card again*?"

He looked up from the globe. "We can talk about it in a minute."

"We can talk about it *now*." Mr. Redla's face was on screen. "Sorry, Mr. Redla, but we had a deal."

"Hi Zoe," Mr. Redla said. "I was just telling Jax I can get your money back if I file a renter's remorse claim. You'll get the cash back within a week and the amount charged to the card will be removed."

I was still mad at Jax, but that could wait. "Thank you so much!" And then I remembered the want ad I saw. "By the way, I'm applying for a job at the Lego Bakery. Can I use you as a reference?"

"Sure." He smiled. Jax was right—he did look like he could be in a toothpaste commercial. "I can do even better than that. When I see the pastry chef this afternoon, I'll let her know you're applying. Did you pick a new name yet?"

"Calypso Bloom."

He chuckled. "Calypso Bloom it is."

It *was* sort of a silly name, but I liked it. "Thank you, Mr. Redla." I waved bye and walked around the desk to where I was off camera but right in front of Jax. And then I gave him my raised-eyebrows glare. He knew exactly what it meant: *this isn't over.* I would have stood there longer just to make sure he got the point, but it was time to make lunch.

Maria and the boys stopped me in the living room and asked me a hundred some questions about the parade.

"I'll tell you what." They looked at me like I was about to announce a prize winner or something—kids are exhausting. "I'm going to make lunch. How about if you set up chairs in front of the window for the parade?"

"Okay, Calypso," Maria said with a goofy smile on her face. "I heard you tell it to Mr. Redla."

Manny tugged on Maria's arm. "¿Qué dijo ella?" (What did she say?)

"Ouch." She pried his fingers off. "Dijo que almorzaremos y luego veremos el desfile." (She said we're going to have lunch and then watch the parade.)

Then they started chanting, "¡Desfile desfile desfile desfile!" (Parade parade parade parade!)

Wishing I had my noise-canceling headphones, I escaped to the kitchen. The menu on the white board said tomato soup, toasted cheese sandwiches and carrot sticks.

At least this will be easy.

I got everything I needed out of the fridge, but before I started to make the sandwiches I washed a stalk of celery. Today when the kids came in begging for food before it was ready, I'd be ready. None of the kids were allergic to nuts, so I filled the celery with almond butter, stuck raisins on top, and cut it into three pieces.

Just then the door chime rang and I almost dropped the knife. Even though I was closer, Jax made it to the door before me and looked through the peephole. "It's both of 'em."

Nooo.

I felt like the wind got knocked out of me. Slash and Burns only rang the chime when they had bad news. "Now what?"

Jax opened the door and Burns came in. "I have a message from the coalition." She took a blue envelope out of her pocket and gave it to me. It was sealed with a circle of wax with a capital *E* in the middle. "Ms. Ella asked me to wait while you read it in case you have a reply."

My hands were shaking. *What in the world could this be about?* Inside the envelope was a note from Ms. Ella and the loan contract we signed with her for two thousand dollars. The contract was stamped, "Paid in Full."

"For real?"

I handed it to Jax.

"The whole two thousand!" He looked amazed. "Why? What's the note say?"

I laid it on the dining room table so we could both read it.

Dear Calypso and Chance,

Jax laughed. "Word gets around *fast*."

We confirmed your suspicion and plan to achieve our goals posthaste. Please stay put until you hear from us.

Sincerely,
E

"Am I dreamin'?" Jax said, shaking his head.

"Crazy, right?" I couldn't believe it.

"What is it?" Maria said.

"The kids are going to get rescued and we're all going home." Even though I was the one who said it, I couldn't believe it. Imagine was a head-spinning mix of nightmares and dreams come true. One day it looks like you might never get home and the next you're packing your bags.

After Maria told her brothers, they all hugged and Maria started crying.

"We did it!" Jax said. He held open his arms. "Bring it in, bad-ass."

And then *I* started crying.

Burns cleared her throat. "Uh, do you have a reply?"

"Tell her we said thank you," I said, but that didn't seem like enough. I still thought it was ridiculous that we had to stay inside—nobody would recognize us with our new colors—but I knew I shouldn't add *that* to our reply. "And that our new résumés will be ready by tomorrow."

Burns nodded. "Got it." She opened the door and Mr. Redla and his daughter were standing in the hall next to Slash, and they were holding picnic baskets.

"Happy Vendredi Gras," she said.

"Wow, what a great surprise," I said. "I'm Zoe. You must be Cheyenne."

"That's me," she said, smiling from ear to ear.

"Good to see you guys," Jax said. "Come on in."

"I'm not staying," Mr. Redla said and handed Jax a basket. "We wanted you to have all the fixin's to kick off festival season, New Orleans-style."

Jax and I talked all over each other thanking him. I couldn't wait to see what was inside those baskets. "Are you sure you don't want to come in?"

"Thanks. I have to get over to the party we're having at the club. I'll see you in the lobby at six, Chey."

"I'll be there." She handed me the basket she was holding and gave him a hug. "Thanks again, Dad!"

As soon as the door closed, she ten-upped Jax. "How'd you figure it out?"

"How'd I figure what out?"

She looked at Maria and the kids. "Um. Does everyone here know about the plan?"

"Not exactly," I said. "Just the goals."

Jax set the picnic basket on the table. "Did you guys get a letter from Ms. Ella, too?"

"No. Dad had a meeting with her this morning. They've known each other forever."

"Really?" I said. "He knew her when she was Cinderella?"

"That's one way to put it." She laughed. "He was the prince."

"No way!"

"So your dad's from Magic Isle?" Jax said. "Can he do magic?"

"Yes and sort of." She tucked a loose strand of purple hair behind her ear. "Not like Ms. Ella, but everyone from Magic Isle can do *some* magic."

"Can *you* do magic?" I said, still trying to picture Mr. Redla as the prince.

"It's in my veins, but I haven't been trained. I might sign up for some demonstrations with Ms. Ella."

"If I had magic, I'd definitely want to know how to use it," I said.

"Then you should sign up."

"Don't you need to have magic?"

Cheyenne opened her mouth and then closed it. "What did Ms. Ella say about how you guys got here? I mean to Imagine?"

"Nothing," I said. "But Fibonacci and Fermat thought me or Jax had magic."

"Well, I don't know for sure, but it used to be that only people with magic in their veins could travel to Imagine from other dimensions."

"Maybe the game changed that some way," I said. I didn't want to be rude, but I knew Jax and I were just ordinary humans.

Jax changed the subject. "So how did your dad end up in New Orleans?"

"If this is going to be a long story," I said, "maybe we should get comfortable." We moved into the living room and Maria followed. The twins were fast asleep on the couch, so we sat on the floor.

"It *is* a long story," Cheyenne said, "but I'll give you the short version."

Maria leaned forward, eyes wide. "Please tell us!"

Cheyenne laughed. "Okay, but it's not that exciting. Everyone on Magic Isle knew the prince was looking for the girl who'd lost her glass slipper at the ball. When he finally found her, he figured she'd accept his proposal and they'd live happily ever after." She smiled the same toothpaste-commercial smile as her dad. "But she said he should have remembered her name or at least her face instead of using her shoe to find her."

"Harsh," Jax said. "I mean, he had to dance with every girl there, didn't he? That's a ton of names and faces."

"It is," Cheyenne said, "but he was so embarrassed and mad at himself for blowing it with Ella that he's never forgotten a name or a face since."

She explained that her dad had wanted a fresh start and wanted to make it on his own, so he gave up his royal title and moved to New Orleans. After he started his law firm, he bought the golf course and Ms. Ella won the contest to design the side nine. She hadn't seen him in twenty years and she didn't recognize him, so he didn't tell her who he used to be until they were friends. "And they've been friends ever since," she said, looking like she thought it was all perfectly normal.

"And your mom's okay with that?" I should have been more polite, but it slipped out.

She laughed again and it seriously sounded like music. *How is that even possible?*

"Mom loves Ms. Ella. They're like sisters." She stood up. "I forgot to tell you that some stuff in the baskets should go in the refrigerator."

Jax and I carried them into the kitchen, and when we opened them, I felt like it was my birthday. One basket had jambalaya, red beans and rice, po'boys, sno-balls, and beignets. The other one had crawfish, gumbo from Dooky Chase, turtle soup from Commander's and a giant King Cake. There were also streamers and shiny bead necklaces in every color. "Oh my God! This is amazing!"

Jax looked at Cheyenne the way a dog looks at a treat. "Yeah, thanks" was all he could come up with.

"Our pleasure," she said. "You guys want to hear some of my favorite bands? I brought my mini globe and speaker."

Suddenly the twins blew into the room like a thunderstorm, poking and pinching each other and stamping their feet so hard they shook the walls.

"Hey, you two ready to party New Orleans-style?" Jax said.

They clapped and jumped up and down even though I'm pretty sure they didn't understand what he said. Manny and Marco were always up for anything Jax suggested.

Cheyenne cranked up the music, and we opened the windows so we could hear the bands down below, too. It was almost as good as being down there. What started out as a depressing day was turning into a party with some of the best food I'd ever had. And Cheyenne was turning out to be cool. Too cool for Jax, that's for sure.

At first I'd wanted to find something wrong with her because she was so together. But we both did gymnastics and we both had Pomeranians, and the more we talked, the more I liked her. But it was still hard not to feel a little insecure around her, so when she said she used to be jealous of *me*, I couldn't believe it. She said she saw me dance at the manor and I was so light on my feet I looked like I was floating. Nobody ever told me *that* before.

When it was time for her dad to pick her up, none of us wanted her to leave, and the twins wouldn't let go of her legs until she promised she'd come back. At least they were finally tired out. When Jax said it was bedtime, they didn't even argue. Maria went to bed, too, and suddenly it was so quiet it felt like the whole day had been a dream.

I was picking up the streamers when there was a knock on the door, and I about jumped out of my skin. I checked the peephole—Burns.

Again?

Jax ran into the living room as I opened the door. Burns just held out another blue envelope with Ms. Ella's wax seal, and Jax took it this time.

"I'll be outside," she said and let herself out.

Jax unrolled the note and held it up so I could see it.

Dear Calypso and Chance,

I'll begin with the good news: Magic Isle authorities have the game master in custody.

"*Sweet!*" Jax said.

It was, but there were a lot more paragraphs that I figured were the bad news.

And now for the bad news: Our technicians don't know how to end the game without harming or possibly killing the avatars. So far, the game master isn't cooperating with them, but Aly has a persuasion plan in the works.

"Aly *can* be pretty persuasive," Jax said.

"I guess."

The New Orleans court won't issue a search warrant for the DeVos manor or an arrest warrant for Master Hoofer without hard evidence. Mr. Redla will take statements from all of you, but they won't carry much weight against someone as wealthy and influential as Ms. DeVos. That said, everyone who has the courage to report a crime can help to make a difference, and it will be good to have an official account of what each of you witnessed.

"That sucks!" I said and smacked the wall.

Jax shook his head. "Sucks all right."

"Everything about this is wrong! Why doesn't the judge want to know what's really happening?"

"Maybe people here take bribes, too. Whatever, it's her word against ours."

"Not if they look at the surveillance tapes or actually search the friggin' place!" I shouted. I wanted to break something.

"Mr. Redla will do what he can to make things right. What else does she say?"

Ms. DeVos has tripled the security force at the manor, eliminating our chances of finding and rescuing the other children. At least for now.

"*Nooo.*" I felt dizzy and had to sit down.

"We really screwed up." Jax sat next to me and we read the last paragraphs.

We can't predict how long this case will go unresolved, so I'm giving you permission to leave the apartment to find work and for other essentials. Always use your current names and only talk when you need to. The animatronic clowns are programmed with voice recognition. If they hear your voices, they will identify you within seconds.

I'm sorry the bad news exceeds the good in this message, but don't lose hope. In Imagine, you'll be lost without hope.

Warmly,

E

Too late. I was already lost.

Nineteen

-△-

JAX

After putting up with Calypso's attitude for three whole days, it was time for a sit-down, whether she wanted one or not. She'd been making the meals she was assigned to make, but that was the only time she came out of her bedroom. Any time I asked her something, she'd just shrug or grunt, and yesterday she lost her shit a little with Maria. After bitching all week about being stuck inside, I figured she'd be the first one out the door, but she wasn't acting like she was planning on going *anywhere.*

When I knocked on her door, I didn't get an answer. Nothing new there.

"Calypso, I need help." The apartment was soundproof, but we were using our new names inside so we didn't screw up outside. She opened the door.

"We're having lasagna tonight and we're out of noodles." She stared at me like I was speaking Chinese. "Do you want to stay with the kids or go to the store?"

"Why can't we use spaghetti?"

"To make lasagna? Girl, you're trippin."

"We can have it with sauce. Skip the lasagna."

"Can I come in?"

She stood there with her arms crossed for a few seconds, and I thought she was going to shut the door, but then she stepped back. The curtains were closed and her bed wasn't made—not good. She pretty much worshipped the sun and said only losers don't make their beds.

"If you're here to lecture me, save it."

"Come on, we're a team."

She frowned.

"Look, I ain't happy either, but when we're down we gotta fight harder."

No response.

"*Damn*, I didn't know you were a quitter." I shook my head to play up my disappointment.

"I'm not a quitter! Every time I get my hopes up, something horrible happens. Every. Single. Time." She turned her back on me.

"It's nice out, you know." I pulled the curtains back and opened the window.

"And that's supposed to make me feel better?"

"It's nice out and Vendredi Gras is in two days. You can go this time."

"Compared to all the ways life sucks, that doesn't add up to much."

"Look, we start with a couple good things. The rest will work out. When shit happens, we just keep our eyes on the prize."

"Are those Mr. Redla's words?"

"Some of 'em." I sat on the rug and she sat down across from me. "When we made up our minds to save Maria and the boys, we knew it was the right thing to do."

"So much for how that turned out."

"Mr. Redla and the coalition are gonna find a way to save all the kids—the ones at the manor and the ones in the game, too. If you don't believe that, why do you even get up in the morning?"

She looked at her unmade bed. "In case you didn't notice . . ."

"I noticed." I waited for her to make eye contact again. "I thought we were in this together. We both wanted to save the kids and get home. *I* still do. You don't believe in this anymore?"

She ran her fingers through her tangled red hair. "What I believe doesn't even matter."

"It does matter. If you stand for nothing, what'll you fall for?"

"Did Mr. Redla say that, too?"

"No. Hamilton said it. To Burr."

"For real?"

I nodded and she finally cracked a smile.

"What if we start with small goals instead of big ones, like taking care of the kids and making a bunch of money to take home. Can you stand for that?"

"I guess so." She stopped combing her hair with her fingers and picked up her brush. "I'll get the pasta."

Score!

I handed her the five I had in my pocket. "The twins are begging to see the tree house, and now that the game master's gone, I can take them over there. Want us to wait till you get back so you can go, too?"

"No. I told Maria I'd be here when she gets back from Ms. Ella's. She's supposed to have her claws turned back into fingernails today, and she wants me to paint them."

"Okay. We won't be out long."

Manny and Marco were waiting for me by the front door. "All right, let's go over the rules." They were picking up English fast. "Rule number one: what are your names?"

"M!"

"M!"

Maria must have been drilling them. "That's right. M and M. Bueno. And what's *my* name?"

"Chance," Manny said

"Oportunidad," Marco said.

"Good job. Are we allowed to wrestle outside this apartment?"

"No. No lucha libre," they said.

"What about talking?"

"No," Manny said, and Marco shook his head.

"That's right. You can whisper, but only if there's something you really need to say, okay?"

They nodded.

"Solid!"

Slash and Burns were out in the hall. "Streets are crowded," Slash said. "We have a robo-cab waiting for us." He led the way to the elevators, and a few minutes later we were in the cab and on our way to the tree house. When the cab dropped us off at the Temple of Gloom, we took the stone path to the tree. Since the coalition had the game master, there were no clowns around, and Slash said we could go in.

Compared with the Swiss Family Robinson Treehouse, this place was a dump. Most of the furniture was broken, and the curtains looked like the rags Zoe used in our volcano eruption. The boys didn't seem to notice how sketchy it was. They were just pumped to be in a tree house.

When we got back down, we took the path along the river to meet the cab, and the mermaids messed with us, asking us our names and trying to guess. Then the redhead pointed at me. "That one smells like the one who was with Zoe."

"¿Está hablando de ti, Jax?" (Is she talking about you, Jax?) Marco whispered.

Then the redhead yelled my name, and the other mermaids started singing "Jax." I started to feel dizzy.

"Crap," Slash said. He picked up the boys, clamped his big old hand around my arm, and booked it through the crowd back to the cab.

"Damn river rats," he said as we got into the cab. "Nothing but trouble."

"Lo siento," (I'm sorry) Marco said.

"It's okay, buddy." I ruffled his green hair. "I can stay out of Riskville."

"Be sure you do," Slash said. His dead serious expression made the hair on my arms stand up.

"Why are they allowed to stay here?"

"They're not allowed." He shook his head. "Nobody knows how to get rid of them. Not even Ms. Ella."

I got chills again and rubbed my arms. *Damn.* "Does anybody know where they came from?"

He grunted. "You should know that one—Earth."

"I thought they were made up." I didn't want him to think I was stupid. "Nobody at home believes they're real."

He nodded and I didn't know what else to say, so I just stared out the window. The streets were more crowded than before, too, so the cab went about as fast as we could have walked. By the time we got to Château Magique, Manny and Marco were half asleep.

Slash took us upstairs, and when the doors opened on our floor, Burns, Calypso, and Maria were standing there.

"We have to go to Ms. Ella's," Calypso said. "Maria told me something about the game that might help get the kids out."

"The boys need a nap. Can you and Maria just go?"

She frowned. "Yeah, but don't you even want to know what it is?"

I didn't think anything Maria said about the game would help Imagine's top techs, but I didn't want to say that. "You know I do."

When we went into the apartment, Calypso laid it out. "When Maria was being trained for the game, one of the avatars showed her safe spaces on the board. Players couldn't detect them there, so they could hide for a few minutes and take a break."

"I don't get it."

"If the avatars all go to safe spaces, maybe the techs can pause the game instead of stopping it. Just for long enough to get them out."

I held both hands up in the air for Calypso to slap. "Ten up! That could work."

Manny copied me and held up his hands, but Marco didn't catch on quick enough and Manny ended up slapping his head, which, of course, made Marco cry. "I gotta get these dudes to bed. Tell Ms. Ella I said hey."

Zoe and Maria were both grinning like it was Christmas morning, but I wished they weren't so psyched. It was a solid idea, but if it didn't work out, they were in for another let down.

Twenty

ZOE

"Is everybody ready?" Slash said.

"Been ready since I got here," Jax said, slinging his backpack over his shoulder.

I pinched my arm to make sure I wasn't dreaming. The safe spaces on the game grid that we told Ms. Ella about last week helped the coalition to rescue the avatars, and almost all the runaway magic was back where it belonged. We were finally going home. I still couldn't believe it.

"We can get the bags," Burns said.

Maria helped Marco and Manny put on their backpacks. "Are you guys ready to go home?"

"Sí," (Yes,) they said at the same time.

"Let's get a move on," Slash said. "There's a big crowd waiting for you at the castle."

"A crowd?" I said as we all headed down the hall to the elevator. "Do you mean the coalition?"

He laughed. "After all this time you still don't know I mean what I say."

After taking the elevator to the lobby, Burns led the way to a long white limo waiting out front. "Ms. Ella wants to send you off in style."

We all got in, and as the limo slowly made its way through New Orleans, I took it all in one last time. I couldn't wait to get home, but I didn't want to forget Imagine or the people we met here. At least, not most of them. The boys were talking nonstop in a mix of English and Spanish, but Jax and Maria were as quiet as I was.

When we passed the DeVos Manor, the windows were boarded up and there were a few guards standing in the empty parking lot. After the avatars were freed from the game, Mr. Redla got a search warrant and the guards found twenty more kids at the manor. DeVos left Imagine on a shuttle before the guards could arrest her, but they got Hoofer. I pinched my arm again, this time hard enough to make my eyes water.

Definitely not dreaming.

After crossing Big Easy Street, we got stuck in a traffic jam right in front of Turtle Terrace.

I can't believe I spent the night in that rat trap.

When we finally started moving again, we only made it a few blocks before traffic came to a complete stop. Slash looked at his watch.

"The ceremony starts in twenty minutes." He got out of the car and looked around. "Total gridlock." We were about a half mile from High Street, and from there the castle was only another quarter mile. "We can walk from here."

Jax agreed, but Maria said the boys couldn't walk that fast, so Slash and Burns decided that Slash would carry the boys, Burns would go with the rest of us, and the limo driver would transfer our luggage to a robo-copter and have it sent to the castle.

As Slash took off carrying Manny in one arm and Marco in the other, we followed Burns as she wove her way through the cars, carriages, and horses. I felt like a mouse trying to get to the cheese in a maze. *Melted* cheese. Between the heat from the cars and the scorching sun, I was burning up. When we made it to the entrance to Magic Isle, sweat was running down my back.

"I sure hope the ceremony's in the shade," I said.

I could have used a break to catch my breath, but Burns picked up the pace. We were sprinting by the time we rounded the corner to High Street. And then suddenly we stopped.

"What the hell?"

Up ahead, Milkshake River was running right up High Street, and dozens of mermaids were splashing around in the water. And then one of them pointed at us.

"Hey, there's Jax!" she said.

They all started chanting his name, and he started walking toward the river like he was in a trance or something. Burns grabbed him.

"Lousy vermin."

She dragged him away from High Street, but the mermaids kept calling his name and he kept looking back over his shoulder. When we were about two blocks away from them, he broke free and sprinted toward the river.

Nooo!

Burns took off after him, and Maria and I followed. She was catching up fast, but he was almost to the river. My stomach felt like it got dropped into a blender.

"Jaaax! Stop!" I yelled as loud as I could.

Just as he looked back, Burns leaped toward him like a football player, and time seemed to slow down.

Please please please catch him.

Then, suddenly, he was on the ground and his hands were in cuffs, but he was still struggling to get away. The mermaids kept singing his name, and he was trying to roll into the river.

"Jax!" I shouted as Maria and I caught up. "You know you'll drown with your hands cuffed."

He looked at me, and it was like he'd just woken up from a dream. He stopped thrashing around. And then he disappeared.

Actually, everything disappeared. There was a flash of light in the middle of High Street that was so bright I couldn't see anything. I squeezed my eyes shut.

What is happening?

When the light faded, I opened my eyes again, and Ms. Ella and Mr. Redla were standing there. Ms. Ella whistled and the mermaids turned to look.

"I sure hope you're enjoying your little excursion," she said with her hands on her hips. "Tonight, we're pulling the last magic tendrils out of Riskville, and that will put an end to your meandering river."

"We don't need the river to meander," the redhead said, and the other mermaids giggled. "Isn't that right, Mr. Club in the Mud?"

Mr. Redla shook his head. "If you say so." He turned to Ms. Ella. "Can we teleport them to the castle?"

"Only two of them have magic."

Wait—what? Which two?

"I know a shortcut through the tunnels," Burns said. "It'll get us there in less than five minutes."

"Perfect," Ms. Ella said. "Lead the way."

Burns led us through an alley and down a dozen concrete steps to an archway leading into a hallway with blue walls. When I looked closer, it looked like marble. At the end of the hall, Burns pushed open a door and we went into a square room with a high ceiling. There were train tracks running through the far end of the room, and they led to tunnels in the walls.

"I think this is the room where the slide dumped me the first day we were here," Jax said.

"Did you take the door hidden in the mirror?" Burns said.

Jax nodded.

"Then this is it." Burns pointed to a round hole in the ceiling above the tracks. "Nobody uses that shortcut except animatrons programmed with train schedules. You're lucky you weren't crushed." Then she pointed to a ladder attached to a wall by the benches. "This will take us up to the main hall of the castle. Who's first?"

"I'll go," Jax said, already starting up the ladder.

"Zoe, you follow Jax and I'll follow Maria," Burns said.

"When you get to the door, give us a holler so we know you made it," Ms. Ella said. "We're going to take the magic shortcut."

I started up the ladder, wondering how far we'd have to climb. My legs already felt rubbery, and thinking about going home made me so happy I felt dizzy—not the best way to feel when you can't even see the rungs of the ladder.

Please don't let there be spiders in here.

If I felt a web on my face, I was going to lose it.

Think positive, think positive.

When my hand reached the knob, I knew I was safe.

Thank you, universe.

Burns was right behind me, and she followed me into the hall. "This way," she said, heading down a side hallway I'd never gone down before. It led to a huge terrace, where Slash was waiting outside the door with the twins. He grinned at me and pointed to the crowd out on the lawn.

"Like I said, a big crowd."

I laughed. I was gonna miss this guy.

The shuttle we were taking looked like the pumpkin carriage Cinderella took to the ball, but without the horses. It was hard to believe something that *untechno* could take us to another dimension. Ms. Ella and the coalition members were standing on a stage next to the shuttle, and Cheyenne and her dad and mom were there too.

Ms. Ella invited us onto the stage and said the ceremony would start with the mayor of New Orleans introducing us as new members of the Legion of Gallantry, whatever that was. "But before we start, our master of financial exchange will give you actual U.S. dollars for the Imagine version."

So many things happened in the past week I almost forgot about the money. "Great! Thank you." Jax and I pulled envelopes out of our backpacks, and I looked around. "Where is she? Or he?"

Ms. Ella walked over to a golden retriever that was wearing a top hat and sitting behind a small desk with a crystal globe. "Money Master, meet Jax and Zoe."

He held out his paw. "It's an honor, Zoe!" he said, lifting my hand up and down with his paw, and then did the same with Jax. "This will only take a minute." I'd heard other dogs talk in Imagine, but not to me. It's definitely trippy to hear a dog say *your* name. "Now, let me check the exchange rate with the U.S." He clapped his paws together. “Good news! Imagine dollars are worth twenty U.S. dollars today.”

“Twenty!” Jax said. “So I’ll be taking home $24,000?”

I couldn’t believe it.

“Correct,” Money Master said. “And Zoe will be taking home $38,400 instead of $1,920.”

“Wow!” Ms. Ella had said the exchange rate would work for us, but she didn’t say how much.

I heard Cheyenne’s musical laugh behind me. “That’s why Dad goes to Earth every year! Cheapest vacation in the multiverse.”

Ms. Ella and Mrs. Redla both burst out laughing.

“You calling me cheap?” Mr. Redla said.

“Of course she’s not, honey,” Mrs. Redla said. “You just can’t pass up a great bargain.”

Mr. Redla grinned. “True.”

“Will we get to see you next time?” Jax said. It was easy to see why he liked Mr. Redla so much.

“Better than that!” Cheyenne said. “You’re invited to my birthday week. And dad said he’ll pay for the shuttle!”

“Dope!”

My head felt like it was being pumped up with helium. *We can come back? Do I even want to?* “Um. Wow. Thank you.”

A mariachi band down in the courtyard started playing, and Manny and Marco jumped up and down.

“Do you kids have any other questions before Mayor Cortez starts the ceremony?” Ms. Ella said.

“Is there anything we need to know about the shuttle?” Jax said.

“Nothing at all. The ride might get a little bumpy, but it’ll get you there. The doors will open in the chemistry lab you teleported from.”

"Ms. Ella," I said, feeling sort of stupid about what I wanted to know.

"What is it dear?"

"We'll arrive with our clothes on, right?"

She giggled. "Well, the first shuttles weren't so reliable where clothes were concerned, but rest assured we fixed that problem. You'll arrive wearing exactly what you have on."

"Ms. Ella," Maria said. "When will you change us back to how we used to be?"

"Right now. Come stand together in a circle."

We crowded together and I held my breath even though I hadn't felt a thing the other times Ms. Ella changed my colors. And I didn't this time either. Ms. Ella waved her hand, and just like that my skin on my arms was brown again, Jax was black and Maria and her brothers were caramel. It was fun to try on the different colors, but when Aly handed me her mirror, it was good to see the face I'd known my whole life.

I noticed that the band had stopped playing, and when I looked up Ms. Ella was stepping to the crystal microphone floating four feet above the stage.

"Welcome to Magic Isle. We have lots of fun in store for you today, and our honored guests are eager to get back home, so we'll keep it short."

The crowd cheered.

"It is my honor to introduce New Orleans's fearless leader and my good friend, Mayor Cortez."

The microphone floated over to the mayor. "Imagine citizens and guests, I'm pleased to announce that the kidnapped children have been rescued and arrangements are being made for their return to their families," she said as Ms. Ella guided Maria and her brothers to the front of the stage. "And the first three are heading home *today*!" Her booming voice echoed off the walls that surrounded the courtyard.

There was more cheering, and this time people threw long-stem purple roses up onto the terrace.

"Master Hoofer," the mayor said, "is in custody and his menacing congress of clowns has been deactivated."

People in the crowd shouted questions, but it was hard to make out what they were saying.

"All your questions will be answered on the globe, but I have a couple of very important announcements to make now." She paused and smiled, stretching out the suspense. "The rules no longer change after dark, so the New Orleans curfew has been lifted!"

If the courtyard had a roof, the crowd noise would have blown it off. Jax and I didn't know the curfew was about the clowns, but it seemed like everybody else did.

"We owe the coalition a major debt of gratitude. And we can shower them with New Orleans hospitality because the magical balance has been restored, and it's safe for all our friends from the Magic Isle to visit us again!"

More cheering.

"And now, it is my great privilege to introduce our two courageous friends, Zoe and Jax."

Ms. Ella nudged us and we walked to the front of the stage.

"Zoe and Jax, for your interdimensional humanitarianism, your innovative thinking, and your incredible bravery, I welcome you to Imagine's Legion of Gallantry!" the mayor said. She took two crystal globes about the size of tennis balls from the table behind her and handed them to us. "Imagine's doors will always be open to you."

We thanked her and she announced that the shuttle would be departing in a few minutes. And then it hit me—it was really time to say good-bye. I felt happy and sad at the same time.

Arthur put my globe in the shuttle and gave me a hug. "You did great, kid," he said.

I managed to say thanks even though my throat was getting tighter every second.

Then Robin hugged me. "Earth's lucky to have you, girl." Lucky to have *me*? I had to swallow the lump in my throat.

Next, Ms. Aly stepped up to me with a giant smile on her face. She took off her crystal heart-shaped earrings and handed them to me. "Remember, Zoe, lead with your heart." The earrings didn't go with my jeans and T-shirt, but I put them on anyway. She wrapped her arms around me and gave me a tight squeeze. "You're the best, girl!"

"*Yeah* she is," Burns said as she ten-upped me, and then Slash swept me up with his ginormous arms and crushed all the air out of my lungs. When he set me back on the ground, Burns handed me a paper shopping bag.

"Should I open it now?"

Slash nodded.

When I looked inside, I couldn't believe it. "Oh my God!" It was filled with beignets. There must have been a hundred.

"Enough to share with your mates," he said.

"Thank you, Slash. Thank you for everything."

When his eyes started watering, I almost lost it, so I focused my attention on Jax instead.

Mr. Redla was telling him about the lifetime club membership he was giving him, and then Cheyenne handed him a box the size of an end table.

"Dad's first law books."

Mr. Redla squeezed Jax's shoulder. "I meant what I said about you considering law school."

Now Jax had tears in *his* eyes. If we didn't leave soon, this was going to turn into a cry fest.

"I'll send you guys a message about my party week," Cheyenne said.

I wondered how, but Jax asked before I could open my mouth.

"On your globes," she said.

"They work?" I blurted.

Ms. Ella was suddenly standing next to me. "Of course they work."

How is that even possible? My head started to spin again.

"Now listen, you two. I've been watching you for almost a month, and you've made me proud." She smiled. "You also made some big blunders, but you learned from them. You both accomplished more than I thought was possible in very little time. You're smart, resourceful and you're brave. But most important, you're kind. All of these traits will take you very far in life, but never forget the basics I taught you."

"Thank you, Ms. Ella," Jax said. He held out his hand but she pulled him in for a hug.

"And you, little lady, never ever allow yourself to lose hope again. Not even for a minute." She held my chin in her hand. "Promise?"

"I promise." Tears started streaming down my cheeks, and I didn't even bother to brush them off.

And then she gave me the longest hug I ever had. "Now get going before I'm too sad to let you leave."

Maria helped Manny and Marco into the shuttle, and then Jax and I got in. Our bags were already inside.

"You'll be there in no time," Arthur said as he made sure we were strapped into our seats. When he patted the outside of the carriage, the door slid shut and we couldn't hear the voices shouting good-bye anymore.

I wished it weren't so quiet. I was going to miss those voices.

Before I could start crying again, the shuttle started to vibrate and I gripped the armrests. I was expecting it to feel like a rollercoaster, but it was more like a rocket taking off. The shuttle started shaking so hard that I started to feel nauseated, but the twins were laughing like it was the best ride they'd ever been on.

Then the shaking stopped as suddenly as it started. The shuttle disappeared and we were sitting on the floor of our chem lab next to our roller bags and backpacks. Jax and I just smiled at each other and stood up.

"And as cold absorbs the heat—"

It was like Ms. Ruoff had seen a ghost. Or two. She stared at us with her mouth hanging open in mid-sentence. When the kids in the class turned around to see what she was looking at, a mix of gasps and screams filled the lab. Maria had to reassure Manny and Marco that they we weren't about to be attacked by a classful of crazies.

"It's us," Jax said, laughing. "How about 'Welcome back'?"

Ms. Ruoff made a beeline to the back of the room. "Where have you been? Who are these children?"

"We'll explain everything," I said, "but first we need to call our moms."

A guy in the back row handed me his phone and somebody handed one to Jax, and we went out into the hall. Ms. Ruoff followed us, still staring at us like we weren't real. I started to punch in my mom's number and realized I had no idea what to say.

"Ms. Ruoff, how long were we gone?"

"Two days," she said. "People have been looking for you since Friday night."

That meant Mom would be terrified but she'd still have hope. I dialed her number and took deep breaths while I listened to the ringer. *Please pick up.*

"Hello," she said. "Is this about Zoe?"

"Mom. This *is* Zoe. I'm okay. I'm at school."

And then we both started sobbing.

Twenty-One

JAX

I'd answered more questions in the last twenty-four hours than I'd answered in my whole life put together. Zoe was being grilled, too, but so far they were leaving Maria and her brothers alone. When our moms said they weren't buying our story, they took us to a trauma therapist, who said we didn't show any signs of being traumatized. I figured that would make things better, but now they thought we were abducted by aliens.

And that wasn't even the worst part. My friends were acting like *I* was an alien, and nobody believed that twenty-four kids were going to show up in the science lab on Wednesday. Ms. Ella wanted us to have temporary foster families lined up before they got here, but that was turning out to be harder than I thought it would be. Since our moms still weren't buying it, today's plan was for Zoe to convince her Aunt Regina that we were telling the truth and for me to convince Chef Liza. But now that I was standing in Santiago's parking lot, I wasn't so sure about this. If she thought I lost my mind, I'd lose my job. But after what those kids went through, they needed people here who would care for them like parents. So I took a deep breath and went in.

When Chef Liza saw me, she got all teary-eyed and gave me a hug. I couldn't believe it.

"Thank God you're okay." She stood back and looked me over. "I heard it on the news but didn't know if it was true until your mom called." She laughed. "Do you know she thinks you were abducted by aliens?"

"Do I know? That's all she's talking about. When I tell her what really went down, she thinks they brainwashed me."

"The story *is* pretty hard to swallow, but as the saying goes, the truth is sometimes stranger than fiction." Chef Liza had a saying for every situation. She walked around me and closed the door to her office. "I want to hear the story from the horse's mouth." She sat in her desk chair and pointed to the chair across from her. "Spill it."

I sat down and told her all of it, from making the volcano explode to the shuttle trip back to the chemistry lab. The only part I left out was the part about the globes working. She didn't ask a single question.

"I believe you."

"You do?" *Is she messing with me?* "Why?"

"I've known you three years and I've never even heard you exaggerate, let alone make up something so trippy." She grinned. "I don't know Zoe, but if your stories match, seems like people are asking you the wrong questions."

"What do you mean?"

"Instead of asking questions you can't answer, like how you got to Imagine or how could magic and mermaids be real, they should be asking what you learned."

She really believed me. I felt like I lost fifty pounds. Like I could float right out of the office.

"But you can't hold it against your moms. They were out of their minds worrying. That'll mess with your head for a while. Give 'em time."

"I hear that, but we need families lined up by tomorrow. If nobody believes us, that ain't happenin'."

She raised her eyebrows. "I eat 'ain't happening' for breakfast."

"What would *you* do? I mean, if you were me?"

"Instead of trying to find twenty-five host families myself, I'd go to organizations that are already set up to help kids."

"Advocates for Kidnapped Kids won't help us if we can't prove the kids are coming. I just figured we'd get the same story from everybody."

She tapped her fingernails on her desk. "Do you have *anything* from Imagine that could be considered proof?"

We had the mini-globes, but we promised each other we wouldn't tell anybody. We were afraid people would steal them or some government dudes would show up and take them. "I have a signed copy of the loan agreement that Ms. Ella forgave. It says 'Imagine' on it, but that doesn't prove the place is real."

She nodded. "Well, for anybody who knows you the way I do, *you* are the proof that something big happened. It's like you got five years smarter in two days." She laughed. "No wonder people are saying the aliens gave you upgrades."

"I'm the same guy I was Friday." Things that happened on Imagine flashed through my mind like a movie on fast-forward. "I just see things differently now."

She smiled and picked up her cell phone. "I'm texting my friend Monica at Children's Services. Maybe there's something she can do without proof."

I checked my phone and saw that Zoe texted me. *G thinks I'm having traumatic delusions. But she'll take in Maria's friend and one more.*

I texted back: *L believes me. She's trying to get Children's Services to help.*

When Chef Liza put down her phone, I set mine on "silent."

"When the kids arrive, they'll have safe homes," she said. "And if they don't arrive, Monica says, and I quote, 'No harm, no foul.'"

I jumped up and held up my hands to ten-up her and then remembered we don't do that here and gave her a fist bump instead.

I thanked her ten or fifteen times and said I'd stay and bus tables for the dinner rush, but she said she had something else in mind. She pulled a book out of her desk drawer and handed it to me—*Sous-Chef: Everything You Need to Know*. "I want you to read this and show up on Monday ready to be a sous-chef."

"Seriously?" I'd make almost twice as much and get to work in the kitchen.

She laughed. "You know I don't joke about my kitchen."

"Whoa! Thanks!" I stuck the book under my arm. "See you Monday!"

On my way home, I wanted to stop at the skate park, but I didn't feel like answering any more questions, so I just went home. When I opened the front door, the smell of vinegar knocked me back.

My mom was standing in the kitchen stirring a spaghetti pot, and pink steam was pouring out of it. It looked like the cauldrons the hawkers in Turtle Town sold.

"I'm home."

"Good. Sit down. We'll eat soon."

I hoped dinner wasn't whatever was stinking the place up.

She stirred the pot and then used the pasta claw to pull out a bright red bra.

What the . . .

"Perfect." She turned to me. "For Cece's shower. White ones cost half as much and dye is cheap." She dropped it in the strainer in the sink and fished out a few more. "This way I can give her four instead of one."

Mom knew more ways to save money than anybody I knew, and when I told her how Zoe and I figured out a budget and that I made money doing math demonstrations, I figured she'd be proud. But she didn't want to hear about any of it. She said the more I talked about it, the more I'd convince myself it was real. She thought the money I brought back was counterfeit.

She opened the oven door and pulled out a large pepperoni pizza with extra cheese. My favorite. "You want to eat in the den and watch the game?"

"Really?" We *always* ate at the table. "You sure you're okay with that?"

"I have five dollars on the Lakers." She grinned. "Besides, it smells better out there."

I took the pizza into the den and she brought the plates. The TV was already on and I changed the channels till I found the game. The Lakers were down by ten at the end of the third quarter.

Having the game on made it easier not to talk, but it didn't stop her from staring at me.

By the time we polished off the pizza, the game was in overtime. "I'll clean up."

"What about homework?"

"I did it."

She narrowed her eyes like she was looking through a keyhole. Then she got up and backed away from me. "Since when do you do your homework before dinner?" She picked up the letter opener on the desk.

Holy shit—she's scared of me.

"Mom, it's really me. I'm not an alien." She just kept holding the opener in front of her like a sword. "I'm just different now. I used to think I didn't have a shot at my dreams." I knew it sounded corny, but I didn't know how else to say it. "Now I know I can do all kinds of stuff. Mr. Redla even said I should think about law school."

Instead of being happy, she started crying. "What are you going to do when those kids don't show up tomorrow? People already think you're crazy."

"They'll show up. Don't—"

She ran into her bedroom and locked the door. She *never* locked that door.

I wished there was something I could do to make her believe me, but at least when the kids got here she'd know that part of the story was true.

The story about kidnapped kids arriving at James Garfield High School was all over the Internet, so I thought there'd be a bunch of news crews, but the parking lot was almost empty, and when I got to the chem lab the only person there was a photographer for the school newspaper. The drivers that Children's Services had lined up weren't even here. I had Monica's number and was supposed to text her when the kids got here.

Zoe showed up a few minutes later.

"Jeez, you'd think at least a few people would be curious," she said and flopped down in a chair near the back of the room. "What time is it?"

"Three minutes till four," Chef Liza said, standing in the doorway grinning. "You didn't think I'd miss *this*, did you?" She sat next to Zoe and introduced herself.

I was too keyed up to sit, so I erased the whiteboards and put the markers away. When I was done, Chef Liza updated us on the time again.

"One minute."

I took a seat behind them and held my breath.

Whooshhh!

A burst of air almost knocked over our chairs and a bright flash of light blinded me. When I could see again, a bunch of kids were sitting on the floor in front of us. The photographer was so blown away she wasn't even taking pictures. She just stood in the middle of the room with her mouth hanging open.

"Welcome back!" Zoe said.

"We're happy you're here," Chef Liza said. "And don't you worry about a thing. We have very nice families who are going to take good care of you until we contact your parents."

A girl about as tall as Maria held up an envelope with Ms. Ella's seal on it. "This is for Zoe and Jax."

"I'm Jax." I walked over and took the envelope.

"I'm Maggie. Is Maria here?"

"Hi, Maggie," Zoe said. "Maria's at my aunt's house. She'll be so happy to see you."

Chef Liza started chatting it up with the kids, and the volunteers who were driving the kids to their host families started showing up a few minutes later. The next forty-five minutes were what she called organized chaos, but it was all over by five o' clock on the dot. She walked out with the last two kids and their driver, and we waved good-bye.

"Open the note," Zoe said as soon as the door closed.

I broke the wax *E* and pulled out a piece of Ms. Ella's stationery. "'See you at seven.'"

"I hope she's right," Zoe said. "Think those globes will really work?"

"I guess we'll find out in a couple hours." I picked up my backpack.

"I'll walk out with you. Are you going to be at home for the meeting?"

"In my room. I'll turn on my gaming music so my mom won't hear what we're saying." The hallway was empty except for a custodian. "You?"

"I don't know. Every time I get on Zoom, I can hear my mom breathing outside my bedroom door. She's convinced I'm not telling her the truth about what happened. So annoying."

We took the stairs down to the first floor, and when we got to the lobby the custodian who we just saw upstairs was sweeping the entryway.

That's impossible.

When we got outside, Zoe grabbed my arm. "*Did you see that custodian*?"

"Yeah."

Zoe looked back over her shoulder and picked up her pace. "Follow me." She took off running through the parking lot and didn't stop till we got to where the buses were parked.

"What's going on?" I said.

"That was DeVos."

"You sure?"

"Totally."

"Great. Now what?"

"Why'd she come *here*?" Zoe said.

"The exchange rate?" If Mr. Redla thought Earth was the best bargain, she could turn her fortune into a mega-fortune here. "We better stick together until we hear what Ms. Ella says."

"Aunt Regina's getting subs from Ed's Market tonight. She won't mind one more mouth."

"Is that place any good?"

"*Seriously*? They're the best subs in town!"

"Okay. Bus or light-rail?"

"Light-rail."

We half-walked, half-jogged to the station, looking back over our shoulders at every intersection.

When we finally got to Zoe's aunt's house, all four kids were on the front porch. Maria and Maggie were making flowers out of tissue paper, and Marco and Manny dropped their toy trucks to rush me. I was glad they were doing good, and Zoe's prediction that the Italian sub would be the best I ever had turned out to be true, but all I could think about was DeVos. It was no coincidence that she showed up at school today, but what was she after? She couldn't get the kids back, and even if she could, she was banned from Imagine. It didn't make sense.

"Earth to Jax," Zoe said. "Did you even hear what I said about *studying*? It's quarter to seven."

Her Aunt Regina came out of the kitchen. "Study here. Vanessa and I are taking the kids to the playground to burn off some energy. She'll be here any minute." And then she pulled down the blind on the front door and winked at me. "We'll be gone at least an hour."

I almost laughed. Zoe said her aunt was always trying to fix her up with somebody, and today I guess it was my turn. But *that* wasn't gonna happen—after Imagine, Zoe was like a sister.

A few minutes later, Vanessa got there and they herded the kids out the door.

Zoe rolled her eyes. "See what I mean?"

This time I *did* laugh. "Can't blame her for wanting you to date someone as fine as me."

"Oh please."

She dug around in her backpack and pulled out her purple globe case, so I got mine out, too, and we set them on the kitchen table. Until then I was sure the globes would work, but now that it was a minute till seven, I *wasn't* so sure.

Come on.

At seven exactly, both globes lit up and Ms. Ella's face appeared. "Howdy!"

Whew. "Hey, Ms. Ella."

"Hi," Zoe said and waved.

"So, 'howdy' isn't what you all say there?"

"Some people say it," Zoe said. "It's just not big in L.A."

"I knew I should have listened to Cheyenne instead of her dad." She giggled. "He set me up." She clapped her hands together. "Well, catch me up. How did it go today?"

I wasn't sure where to start.

"All the kids are in safe homes," Zoe said. "Nobody believed they were coming, but Jax convinced his boss and she got Children's Services to help."

"Good job! I knew you'd find a way. Are your authorities looking for the kids' parents?"

"Starting tomorrow," I said. "We wanted to give them a night before people started asking them a bunch of questions."

"Good thinking. I'm very proud of you and very grateful. We all are." But she didn't sound happy. "I'm sorry to say I have bad news." She sighed. "You wouldn't happen to have swings nearby, would you?"

We shook our heads.

"The engineers were able to retrieve the shuttle log from DeVos's flight." She frowned. "She's on Earth."

"We know," Zoe said. "She was at school today, dressed like a custodian."

Ms. Ella gasped. "Already?"

"What do you think she wants?" I said.

"There's only one thing that horrible woman wants when she doesn't get her way." She shook her head. "Revenge." She tapped her fingers on her desk. "She wanted you to see her today or she'd have stayed out of your way."

The hair on my arms stood up. "Just great."

"What should we do?" Zoe said.

"Get out your notebooks."

For the next fifteen minutes, she filled us in on the damage DeVos had done in other dimensions and what her favorite tactics were. I wasn't surprised that big bribes were on the list. I wondered how much her billions were worth here on Earth. "Did Money Master change money for her before she left?"

"No, but the shuttle she took has an AEM—automatic exchange machine—so it won't be long before she has as much influence there as she had here." She sighed again. "I wish I'd have taught you some magic while you were here."

"Magic?" I thought I might have heard her wrong.

"Ms. Ella," Zoe said. "Is it true that we couldn't have transported to Imagine without having some magic?"

She smiled. "Yes, but don't go getting big heads about it. A whole lot of people have some magic. What Fibonacci and Fermat said when you arrived was true. One of you had to have magic to teleport into Imagine. As it turns out, you both have some."

"Does that mean we can end up in Imagine again, like what happened last time?"

"Now that we shut down the game, that sort of thing probably won't happen again."

"Probably?" I said.

Ms. Ella smiled. "Sorry, Jax, but when magic and reality mix, things aren't always predictable." She tapped her fingers on her desk.

"But that doesn't explain why we have magic to begin with," Zoe said.

"The short, simplified answer is that everything alive starts out with at least 10 percent magic, including human beings. But by the time most people grow up, their connection with it is so thin they can't use it anymore."

"On High Street when the mermaids were trying to take Jax, you told Mr. Redla that you couldn't transport us to the castle because only two of us have magic. Why doesn't Maria have magic? She's not grown up yet."

"The answer to that question is a sad story, Zoe." She took a sip from her glass. "Most kids Maria's age still have magic, but a lot of times kids who are traumatized or have it tough at home stop believing in the magic. Manny and Marco didn't have the same experience as their sister, so their magic is still working."

"Can we help Maria's to work again?" Zoe said.

"I'm so glad you asked." Ms. Ella clapped her hands together. "Teaching magic on the globe isn't ideal, but we'll make it work."

"You're going to teach Maria magic?" Zoe said.

Ms. Ella giggled. "No. *You're* going to teach her after I teach you."

"For real?" I couldn't believe we even had magic, and now we were going to learn how to use it?

"For real. But before you do any substantial magic, you need to accept and practice the responsibility that comes with it."

Am I hearin' this right?

"The first few months we'll focus on helping the kids who were avatars to strengthen their connections with their magic."

"What about DeVos?" I said.

"She doesn't have any magic left, but she'll find other ways to cause trouble for you. Managing this situation will mean using magic along with everything you learned on Imagine. Magic alone is rarely a good way to solve a problem, and it's the laziest way to create things, so it's not nearly as fun or fulfilling as using our brains."

I never thought of that, but it made sense.

Then she told us we'd both be meeting with her one hour a day until she was sure we could use our magic well enough to protect ourselves, and then it would be twice a week. I'd meet with her in the mornings right after Mom left for work, and Zoe would meet with her after school.

"Ms. Ella," Zoe said, looking more serious than I'd ever seen her. "DeVos knows what school we go to, so she probably knows where we live. What if she tries something tonight?"

"We sent guards to look for her, but she's never easy to find. Slash will be trailing you, and Burns will trail Jax, but don't talk to them or act like you know them."

"Okay," Zoe said.

Good to know they had our backs.

"One more thing," Ms. Ella said. "When we meet tomorrow, I want you to answer the question 'What would I most love to contribute to the universe before I die?'" She smiled. "And remember what you learned about limitations being illusions. I want to hear about the biggest, boldest contribution you can imagine. Got it?"

"Got it," I said.

Zoe nodded.

"Okay then, sweet dreams." Her face vanished and the globes went back to looking like paperweights.

Zoe frowned. "I have no clue what I want to contribute."

I had some ideas, but I wasn't ready to tell anybody. "I think it has to do with what we care about most. Like Hamilton asking, 'What will we stand for?'"

"Nobody ever asked me that. I never thought about it, did you?"

"A little." I wasn't worried about coming up with an answer for Ms. Ella, but I *was* wondering how I'd get my grades up, work at the restaurant and fit in magic lessons.

We put our globes back in their cases.

"Now we definitely can't tell anybody about these," Zoe said. "I've wanted to be able to do magic ever since I read Harry Potter." She was smiling like she just won the Powerball. "Aren't you excited?"

I definitely wasn't excited. "It's a big responsibility. Plus an hour with Ms. Ella every day and time to practice is a lot to fit in."

"True." She put her globe case in her backpack. "And helping all those kids is going to take a ton of time. And *patience*."

Helping the kids was the part that sounded best to me.

That's it.

I knew the answer to Ms. Ella's question: I wanted to help kids who'd lost their connection to magic to get it back.

"Ready to go?" Zoe said. "I can lock the door from the inside."

We went outside, and Slash and Burns were standing on the other side of the street.

"See you tomorrow," I said, making sure I didn't look right at them.

"See ya."

She turned the corner and Slash crossed the street to follow her. As I went the opposite direction, I wondered how many times Slash and Burns had been to Earth. And how many other people from other dimensions are here without us knowing it.

A few guys I recognized were boarding in the bank's parking lot, but I still had to study for Friday's math test. They started hassling me, trying to distract me from what I needed to do, and without looking back I knew they were checking out Burns. If I told them she was my guard, there was no way they'd believe it. And a week ago I wouldn't have either. I wouldn't even have been able to *imagine* it.

Turns out Ms. Ella was right. What we believe and what we can imagine change everything.

Jax Robinson

1001 Wanderlust Blvd., New Orleans, Imagine|
Globe: Jax@MsElla.ChâteauMagique

1. Objective

To help children from the ages of 8 to 13 to excel in math and encourage them to appreciate how valuable math skills are for lifelong success

2. Education

Freshman: James Garfield High School
College Preparatory
Focus: Math & Science

3. Skills & Abilities

LEADERSHIP

Lead team of 12 lifeguards
Train new table bussers at four-star restaurant
Organize Toys for Tots collection on my street

TEACHING

Tutor middle school math students
Teach skateboarders new tricks
Assist with teaching beginner swimming class

4. Experience

TABLE BUSSER | SANTIAGO'S | FEBRUARY 2019–PRESENT

Set tables, place and replace silverware, fill water glasses, clear and clean tables, chairs and dining room floor

HEAD JUNIOR LIFEGUARD | YMCA | MARCH 20, 2021–PRESENT

Train and lead new lifeguards ages 12 and 13

Sports & Hobbies

- COMPETITIVE SKATEBOARDING
- AMATEUR BOXING
- GAMING

5. Community Service

6. YMCA: math tutor

7. TOYS FOR TOTS: annual toy collection

8. References

Liza Lopez, chef, Santiago's

Others available upon request

Zoe Martinez

1001 Wanderlust Blvd., New Orleans, Imagine |
Globe: Zoe@MsElla.ChâteauMagique

1. Objective

To work in a spa or club, where I can teach gymnastics or dance to children from the ages of 9 to 12

2. Education

Freshman: James Garfield High School
College Preparatory
Focus: Health & Culinary Arts

3. Skills & Abilities

TEACHING

Work with young gymnasts to improve their basic skills
Assist teacher in dance classes

COMMUNICATION

Report and write feature articles for school newspaper
Zoelicious TikTok about great food

4. Experience

SCOOPER | GELATO HEAVEN | HOLIDAY HELP

2018–2020

Greet customers, offer them samples and fill their orders

DOG WALKER | APRIL 20, 2021–PRESENT

Walk, feed and water neighbors' dogs

Sports & Hobbies

- COMPETITIVE GYMNASTICS
- DANCE
- FOODIE

5. Community Service

6. VOLUNTEER: Monthly Neighborhood Improvement & Cleanup

7. References

Available upon request

Michael Alder, Esq.

Michael Alder is a champion for the underdog both inside the courtroom and out. Owner and senior trial attorney at AlderLaw, he generously supports other trial attorneys, charitable causes, and the greater Los Angeles community.

Michael offers free seminars, presents *AlderTalk Live* on Instagram and YouTube, maintains a free nine thousand deposition database and expert witness directory, and mentors young lawyers as well as offers them access to his archived depositions and financial assistance through the AlderLaw Warrior Fund program.

A strong believer in giving back, Michael is on the board of trustees for the Inner City Law Center, a pro bono law firm dedicated to ending homelessness and advocating for veterans' benefits. He also serves on the board of directors for the National Hispanic Media Coalition and the Metro Los Angeles YMCA. He is a founder of the American Museum of Tort Law and a founder and board member of Los Angeles Trial Lawyers Charities, a nonprofit public benefit corporation organized to improve the lives of those in need in Southern California.

In his spare time, he enjoys relaxing at the family's Louisiana ranch, exercising, gardening, raising chickens and goats, and entertaining family and friends.

AlderLaw.com
ZALawyers.com
YouTube: AlderTalk

Gina Zapanta-Alder, Esq.

Gina Zapanta-Alder is a passionate advocate for the East Los Angeles community and the Greater Los Angeles Latinx community. Co-founder and attorney at ZapantaAlder Law, a workers' compensation firm, she's committed to supporting and defending those who need it most. She and Michael Alder have established a $100,000 endowment at Loyola Law School, to be awarded to a first-generation Latina. They also founded ZAgives, a 501(c)(3), which has contributed more than $90,000 to local restaurants, health care staff, and grocery store employees during the COVID-19 pandemic. They hosted a "Day of Giving" at the Weingart-East Los Angeles YMCA, which provided more than twelve thousand meals, ten thousand toys, and eight thousand home deliveries.

Gina has also partnered with author and educator Stedman Graham to deliver his Identity Leadership program to inner-city students and is developing strategic alliances between Stedman Graham Enterprises and the Latinx community.

She is a member of the Los Angeles Latino Chamber of Commerce and the University of Southern California Latino Alumni Association's Corporate Advisory Council. She also serves on the boards of Children's Hospital Los Angeles, Adventist Health White Memorial, and Monterey Park Hospital and is board secretary for the Los Angeles County Employees Retirement Association.

Gina enjoys entertaining, traveling, dancing, and learning Mandarin Chinese with her daughters.

ZALawyers.com

Acknowledgments

Thank you to the cabdriver whose story about writing a book to help kids navigate life inspired us to write this one.

To the students and parents who took our survey, thank you for the valuable input about the story and what you wanted our main characters to learn.

To Toni Robino and Doug Wagner of Windword Literary Services, thank you for creative development and editing.

To our beta readers, Madysen McConnell, Natalia Marquez, and Camila Marquez, thank you for your enthusiasm and advice.

To Mark Veon, thank you for your help with the skateboarding scene; to Matthew Baganz, thank you for proofreading; and to Cecilia Rinaldi, thank you for translating the English into Spanish. To Arianna Nicora, thank you for the map of Imagine.

To the team at Mascot Books—Naren Aryal, CEO; Austin Ross, Production Editor; Matthew Gonsalves, Graphic Designer; and Kristin Perry, VP of Operations—thank you for helping us to share this book with the world!

To our readers, remember that what you believe and what you can imagine change everything! Thank you for taking the journey with us and for using what you learn to excel and help others.